LUCKY DUCK

LUCKY DUCK

at the mall. in the 80s. with a dog.

Mike Garretson

 Torchflame Books
Vista, CA

ISBN: 978-1-61153-509-9 (paperback)

ISBN: 978-1-61153-511-2 (ebook)

ISBN: 978-1-61153-649-2 (large print)

Library of Congress Control Number: 2024922004

Lucky Duck is published by: Torchflame Books, an imprint of Top Reads Publishing, LLC, 1035 E. Vista Way, Suite 205, Vista, CA 92084, USA

The publisher is not responsible for websites or social media accounts (or their content) that are not owned by the publisher.

Cover design and interior layout: Jori Hanna

To that memory of an Orange Julius in one hand, a bag of newly purchased records from Sam Goody in the other, and the swirling aromas of the food court wafting over you as you run into some friends at your local mall.

CHAPTER ONE
THE BUZZER

For me, good luck first arrived every morning at the breakfast table. It came in the form of my mom reading the *Wichita Eagle Beacon* to me while I downed my Rice Krispies before heading to school. If I were to tell this story starting at the end, you'd be reading about me walking out of my lawyer's office. If I were to start in the middle, it would likely commence with the day I robbed the bank. Or, if I chose to start at the beginning, I think it would be the day I made a basket, and the referee decided my jump shot occurred after the buzzer. I guess I'll start at the beginning.

I've got to be the luckiest guy in the—oh, I was going to say the entire world, but make it the Northern Hemisphere, I don't want to embellish and lose you right off the bat. Lucky? Not only because I was born into a typical American middle-class family, but I was also able to go to college, get a few decent jobs, and raise a family and all that. I did get away with robbing a bank—and all in all, I don't think it changed my life that much.

Yep, you read that right: I robbed a bank. I got away with it. It wasn't even that hard. Some luck was involved in the aftermath, for sure. It was nice to be absent of money worries like most kids after college, but it wasn't like I was flying around in jets and going to the World Series one night in Los Angeles and a rock concert in London the next. I've been able to live a normal life.

This topic of luck can be a prickly one. Some people can list every negative thing they've ever encountered and chalk it up to bad luck. I've always felt like I landed on the good luck side of things. I remember in high school, in my favorite history class, and this teacher loved to play current event games every Friday. He would set up his blackboard kind of like a game of Jeopardy, and I would win almost every week. Did I win because I was the smartest? No way. Absolutely not. There were at least six kids in there who roasted me on the ACT test. But their moms didn't read the newspaper out loud at the breakfast table every morning to them.

"Oh, here's a story about the Middle East," Mom would say. Or, "Joel, don't leave yet. I want to read this story to you about new scientific findings. It's all about DNA."

I knew who many world leaders were and which countries they led. Names like Thatcher, Trudeau, Menachem Begin, Anwar Sadat—they didn't even phase me. I knew who was winning the Oscars and the Nobel Prizes, and I knew who the ranking senators were and who the speaker of the House was (Tip O'Neill if you want to google it). So, it wasn't an intelligence thing—it was just luck. Luck that my mom loved to read the *Wichita Eagle Beacon*, *Newsweek*, or *Time* magazine to me over her coffee and my sugared-up Rice Krispies, and luck that Mr. Cole loved to play current event games with his junior history classes. So, what if I won the current event games? Why does that make me lucky?

Well, Mr. Cole was the head of the Eisenhower Scholarship Committee for the county, and according to our guidance counselor, Mr. Cole thought I showed a lot of leadership potential, and she said that I should "most definitely thank him for his support." The way she said it—and it was the only time the guidance counselor and I spoke in four years of high school—she appeared to be amazed that anybody would think I was "Eisenhower material," as it was a major scholarship our county offered. I'm sure she hadn't been impressed with my meager 3.1 GPA and barely above-acceptable ACT score (but for the record, I had a hangover when I took that college entrance exam after drinking hard liquor for the very first time the night before).

Where does all this luck lead to? Well, the Eisenhower scholarship changed the math of my college decision. I was planning on going to Kansas State University and taking advantage of all that tax money that must have been pouring into the state university system because tuition in 1983 was $23 per credit hour. That comes out to $345 per semester. Now that I had the Eisenhower scholarship—$2,000 per year, renewable for eight semesters—I could investigate attending a private college. Private college? For the rigorous curriculum and prestigious faculty? Nope. Attending a small, private college would allow me a chance to keep playing basketball. Three or four of the small colleges in Kansas and a couple in Nebraska had sent me literature and called me on the phone a few times. I loved playing ball, and with my average skills and size (six foot two), there was no way a big college was going to offer me a scholarship or even a spot as a walk-on. Anyway, the $2,000 per year in scholarship money made the expensive, small colleges now within range. A summer job would pay for most of the rest, and I'd borrow about $500 per year for room and board and some extras, but I felt lucky to be able to go to college, play some basketball, and not have to bother my parents for any money to go to school.

Choice of schools? Once again, I came out on the lucky side of things. I chose Kansas Wesleyan University in the town of Salina, right smack dab in the middle of Kansas. Why was this a lucky choice? Well, because our basketball team wasn't very good, which meant that I got to play some. Now, these are not the college games you ever saw on ESPN or any other sports network that covers NCAA games. There are hundreds of these small colleges, they belong to what they call the NAIA, and these colleges might have anywhere from four hundred to four thousand students at their schools. I got to play a few minutes here and there during my freshman and sophomore years. In my junior and senior years, I started a handful of games, but most of the time, I came off the bench. I usually scored four or five points a game, but one night near the end of my senior year down at Southwestern College in a dark old cavern of a gym, I had nine points and put up the last shot of the game. We were down by about fifteen points, so it didn't matter anyway, but the other nine guys and I were playing hard out there, trying to show our coaches that we were worthy of more minutes when the score of the game *did* matter. Anyway, I put up an off-balanced jumper from the corner, which left my hand about a full second before the buzzer. Swish! Ah! An excellent way to end the game for me—and then the ref on the baseline waves his arms and calls it: no shot. It would have been my only collegiate game in double figures, and if you got double figures, you got your name in the *Salina Journal* the next day. Your name would appear in the write-up about the game, not just the box score. I clipped the box score with all the last names and total points scored. There I was, *Howard, 9,* among *Wagner, 24; McNeil, 16; and the rest.* I saved that thing for probably ten years, but I didn't bother clipping the story due to some flailing arm ref who wiped out my moment. So, where was my luck that day? Turns out the ref may have done me a nice little favor—I will let you decide on that one.

After that game at Southwestern—and I want to emphasize one more time, that shot left my hand well before the buzzer, and the box score should have said *Howard 11*—anyway, after Southwestern, we had one more home game, and we didn't make the playoffs, so my basketball days were over and the only thing left for me was to graduate, get a job, and get on with my life.

Before I graduated, I needed a part-time job because I was seriously low on dough. It was very common for me to have anywhere from five to eighteen dollars in my checking account before shoveling some snow, reffing some games at the Y, or helping a furniture store move some stuff in or out of a warehouse to earn some cash. The bank account would swell to maybe as much as thirty or forty bucks, and then a little gas and some late-night stops at the Kwik Shop or Burger King would deflate my account back to its customary low levels.

Salina had a brand-new mall, so I took a stroll in search of a store in need of some part-time help. It was 1987, and the mall was a busy place. From the mall walkers in the early morning to moviegoers enjoying the late show, malls were a huge piece of the American economic machine in the '80s and '90s in middle America. Almost every storefront was occupied, and nearly every store was fully staffed. It was rare, but sometimes you'd see a Help Wanted: Apply Within sign.

I sauntered past the food court with its trademark smells of cookies, hot dogs, pizza, and the always-beckoning, fresh-popped caramel corn. I veered into a bookstore for a moment or two and looked at posters and some coffee table-type books featuring nature and sports scenes. They were out of my price range, and I didn't have a coffee table either, but hey, the photography was incredible. Right next door to the bookstore was a Kinney Shoes, and I did need a new pair, or even two pairs, of shoes—but a job would have to come first.

Quickly appearing from the backroom came a face I seemed to faintly recognize. He was carrying two boxes of shoes and headed for a mom who had her three little ones with her. The boxes were covering up his name tag as my mind was quickly trying to go through the files in my brain to come up with where I had seen this guy. I didn't want to rudely peer into his face and say, "Do I know you?" but I did slowly lean his way, and when he lowered a box, his nametag read "MANAGER—David." Hmm, I was hoping a name would jolt my brain into pairing a face with a name and a time and a place with an association, and it would be, "Oh, that guy coaches a kids' team at the Y," or some similar problem-solved feeling of accomplishment.

"Someone will be right with you," Manager David said in my direction.

I started to say, "I'm just looking," but just nodded and kind of started browsing around. There were probably five or six places in the mall where I could get shoes, but what I was actually looking for was a Help Wanted sign. I strolled past the cash register, a likely place for a Help Wanted poster, and when I didn't see one, I headed for the door to stroll down the mall's long corridors in search of a job, and then I heard Manager David say, "Hey, Joy, can you help this customer here? This big fifth grader of hers has a program tomorrow night, and he needs some dress shoes."

I saw a blonde worker—Joy, I assumed—stride over to help with that transaction, and Manager David hustled across the store to cut me off before I could get past the edge of the industrial metal gate that would slide shut at the end of the business day. He clearly didn't want me to get out of the store without providing me service, and I felt a little bad. *Well, Manager David, I don't think you have any shoes for under $7.39, so I really need to move on.*

"Hey, you're Joel, aren't you? Joel Howard from Wesleyan?" His voice had gone from shoe salesman to interested info-seeker.

Now my mind was locked down in fast-forward mode. *How does this guy know me?* As I was wheeling through possibilities, he interrupted my bullet train of images and thoughts, grabbed me with his eyes, and said, "You play for the basketball team. I've seen you play a few games."

Man, I felt like a star right then. Mr. Local Celebrity. Even five seconds of fame can make a guy feel pretty good.

"Actually, I've only seen a couple of games this year. Mrs. O'Hara, the cheerleaders' sponsor, she's my wife. I went down to Southwestern last Saturday. Man, that's a brutal drive," he stated.

That's where I had seen his face! He was sitting just a few rows above the bench with his wife . . . and then our minds melded for a brief moment.

"Hey," Manager David O'Hara said, "there is no way that buzzer went off before you shot that last one in! That was a rip-off!"

Thank you! I wanted to shout out loud. Now call the *Salina Journal* and tell them to put my name in the paper: *Also in double figures for the Coyotes was Joel Howard with eleven points, quite possibly the greatest eleven points ever scored since Mr. Naismith invented the game of basketball.*

He was saying something about how he promised to go with his wife to more road games this year, but he was too busy with the store, and I could hardly focus on what he was saying because a memory of a game earlier in the season popped into my mind and his voice just faded into the background.

We were in a huddle with under a minute to go, and Coach B was drawing up an inbound play on a legal pad—this is way before those fancy whiteboards or magnet boards all the teams have now. Coach was furiously drawing and talking as fast as he could, and he looked up at our top scorer, Allen Wagner, and said, "Allen, quit staring at Mrs. O'Hara and pay attention to this play."

Well, Allen hit the shot, we won the game, and pretty much the rest of the year, anytime somebody wanted to break the silence or crack a little joke, they would begin with, "Allen, quit staring at Mrs. O'Hara and pay attention."

Manager David continued to talk to me about basketball, and

I continued to drift in and out of the conversation, thinking about his wife off and on. In those days, she was what we called a "brick house," whereas today, she might be referred to as "a hottie with a body."

". . . and that gym. Run down and dark. Darkness doesn't explain why the ref couldn't hear a buzzer, though . . ."

Blonde Joy had finished getting the little lad his dress shoes. She was checking on another couple that had come in just before closing time, and David still wanted to talk basketball. I wanted to check out a few more places before everyone closed up for the night, so I gently tried to ease my way out of the conversation and the store.

"Well, Mr. O'Hara, I better let you get back to your store. I was kind of walking through the mall tonight hoping I would find a place that needed a part-time worker," I admitted.

"Dang. Joel, I wish I could help you out there, but I've got a stack of job apps in my office . . ."

And then, it was like I could see something in his eyes. I could see him thinking, *Ah, man, this kid just got ripped off by some goofy referee. He needs a little . . . a little good luck to come his way.*

"You know, Joel," David propped one foot on one of those "try-on" stools they have in shoe stores and leaned forward. "I could start you out slow. It wouldn't be many hours for the first couple of weeks. One of my part-time guys just told me he's going to be moving on soon. Got him a job at the radio station. Sports guy, so he won't be able to work evenings.

"I could slide you in on some nights and weekends," he continued.

"That works for me," I said.

And that was just luck.

So now tell me. If the ref gave me my two points, and I got my name in the paper, would Manager David have ever given me that part-time job ahead of the stack of job apps in his office? Nothing about that game would have stuck in his head except maybe that brutal van ride he mentioned. It might have been just a nod and a "Come by anytime. We've got a great selection of sneakers." Nope, I'm 100 percent sure that when the ref decided that buzzer beat my shot, it was pure luck. Good luck. Good luck for me.

Where's the luck in getting a mall job selling shoes?

That mall had a bank.

I robbed that bank, and I got away with it. On Black Friday in 1987.

CHAPTER TWO
NEE NEE

Her name was Nadine Blass, but I called her Nee Nee. I grew up in a family that just seemed to pour out nicknames on people like Johnny Appleseed planted apple trees across the American countryside. One neighbor, who liked to water his lawn during a rainstorm, was Waterhog. Another neighbor, who shared his garden liberally, was Tomato Tom (his real name was Gordon). Dad called the lady across the street Mrs. Green because she had a green car. When she died and Mom saw her obituary, she shrieked, "Oh, my stars! I've been calling her Mrs. Green right to her face!" Dad and I got a good chuckle out of that.

Nadine was my girlfriend through the last couple years of college. Her nickname came about in a typical way for me. After one or two dates, I think I was calling her Nadeeny for a while, which morphed into Deeny and then Nee, which became Nee Nee, and that was that.

Nee Nee was from Boston. Kids who go to small colleges come from all over the United States, and the world really. And the one question they never ask each other, but the one question everyone else always seems to ask them, is, "How in the world did you wind up at 'School X' when you came from [insert city, state, or country name]?" The reason the kids never ask the question is that we all just tell each other straight up, and there's never a "Really?" or "You gotta be kiddin'?" The answer is as individual as your fingerprint, but the solution behind it is that, for some reason, the pull or the push of "School X" was presented at just the right time, and a decision was made to go to a college you had never really even heard of.

My pull was being able to be part of a basketball team—to get to brag a little that I played college basketball, which leaves out the whole story that I was already thinking about leaving the team and the school when the last game before Christmas break my sophomore year, two guys got in a little trouble with the law, got sidelined, and I got to start a game. That little bit of ego-flooding serotonin—being announced as one of the five starters, being on the court when the ref tossed the ball in the air—was like a hit of an addict's favorite drug. I was hooked, and I was staying at Wesleyan no matter what, just in the hope of another hit.

For Nee Nee, it was a push. The push was her family. The first time we truly talked, she told me it was her desire to play some college tennis, but when I visited her and stayed with her family one spring break, it was obvious she wanted to get far away from home. I'm surprised Kansas was far enough. A form letter with a nice brochure picturing a few smiling kids walking down a campus sidewalk to just the right high school student on just the right day, with just enough motivation to venture out to a place unknown, and hundreds of kids will flock and share their experiences.

Nee Nee was a good girlfriend. She was always kind to others and usually kind to me—even when we broke up a couple of times—and 99 percent of the time, she was the smartest person in the room. Not in a trigonometry or biochemistry smart way, but in the way that she could always read a room and diagnose people, motives, and social situations. She could be at a party for an hour and say one sentence that was the most definitive and precise statement of the entire night. People would pause, nod, and after a second or two of silence, go right back to their party-talk. She would usually refrain from further banter, as if to say, *I have spoken*, with just the right sentiment. It was kind of mysterious, and, looking back on it, it was dang sexy.

Nee Nee and I were not together by the time I robbed the bank, or there is no way I would have ever advanced that plan in my mind beyond the "Whoa, that's some crazy-think" stage of mental operations that later formed into physical acts.

I always felt sort of special to have Nee Nee at my side through my last couple of years at Kansas Wesleyan. She would come to almost every basketball game, and she was a good sport about sitting around and playing cards with some of my friends when she was the only girl in the apartment. This exposed her to gross talk, not to mention the sounds and smells four to six guys would generate while sitting around eating chips and dip and drinking pop or beer.

I proofread a few of the papers she wrote for her classes. I'd go over to her place, and even though it was in a basement, it was always immaculately neat and smelled nice from a scented candle or a woven basket of potpourri. She was a biology major with a teaching minor. Nee Nee would take her faultlessly typed paper out of a neatly labeled folder and insist I look for spelling or grammar errors, and I don't remember ever finding hardly any.

"Do you see any misspelled words, Joel?" she'd ask earnestly.

"The next one I find will be the first," I'd say, trying to be clever.

If I suggested any changes or edits, she would rarely take my advice, usually saying something like, "I had it that way in my rough draft, but I like this better." I think it was more polite than saying, "Wrong."

One paper she wrote for a human anatomy class was on the topic of blushing. She went into all the science about corpuscles and blood vessels and white cells and all kinds of sciency stuff. It was this extremely technical discussion of the function of blushing, but the part I found interesting was that humans can't control their blushing. It's a response to a stimulus that sparks a reaction we can't reject. Humans can do some amazing things, like slow their heart rate down to a ridiculously low number of beats per minute. Humans can hold their breath for, I don't know, maybe fifteen or more minutes underwater. Humans can lift insane amounts of weight, run or swim really fast, climb vertical rock walls, and train their bodies to do amazing feats. But we can't defeat the blush.

I wanted her to emphasize that the stimuli were random and could not be predicted. One stimulus might cause Person A to blush but the very same stimulus for Person B would cause no response at all. And the fact that a blush cannot be faked! I found that to be maybe the most interesting part of the whole phenomenon.

"You need to emphasize that," I excitedly told Nee Nee, thinking I had the key to her getting an A on her paper and at least one wing of Peters Science Hall being named after her.

"It's a biology paper, Joel, not some feel-good psychology paper. Let's stick to the biology," Nee Nee said as she looked over her neatly organized notes.

"Anytime I'm around you, I'm *thinking* about biology, Nee Nee," I said, with a coy motive in my voice.

And SHE BLUSHED. NEE NEE BLUSHED.

She tried to deny it, but those red splotches up her neck would not let her. I laughed, and then she finally laughed. She stacked her notes and the final draft neatly into a folder, making sure things would be orderly when she opened the folder again.

Then she moved toward me, and we were first lovingly and then passionately intimate. It wasn't the first time, but it was the best time. I owed it to a blush. One sudden and unpredictable and wonderful blush.

I only went to a few of her tennis matches, one of which became the genesis of our final break-up. I lived in a three-bedroom apartment with anywhere from three to five other guys, and she rented a basement room from an older lady who required some assistance. It wasn't the best setup for us to be a devoted couple. Nee Nee's old lady housemate, Mrs. Kimball, forbade overnight guests, but I'd stay over secretly sometimes. Feeling like you're sneaking around is just not a very relaxing mode to operate in full-time. I remember joking to my room-mates, "If the ol' gal that Nadine watches over ever kicks the bucket, I will be outta here shacking up with Nee Nee before the old lady's body comes down to room temperature."

"The ol' gal" figures into part of my good luck scenario and the bank robbery—and since you're wondering, $138,038 exactly. That's how much cash I got from the bank. It's an easy figure for me to remember for some reason.

The ol' gal wanted Nadine to take her to the wedding of a great-niece or shirttail cousin or some relative down the road, about sixty miles away. So Nee Nee persuaded me—after assuring me the ol' gal would pay her a nice sum—to go along for the ride on a nice spring afternoon to a small country church in the middle of Kansas for the wedding of two people I would never see again. The ol' gal did pretty well for herself that day. She just needed a walker to get from place to place, and the church had a nice, smooth ramp and accommodating double doors, so getting her inside for the wedding was no problem. The reception was outdoors under a tent, and the uneven ground was a concern, but Nee Nee was excellent at getting me and two other guys to make sure the ol' gal had a safe place to sit and enjoy her cake and punch.

While most everyone else was inside the tent telling family stories and dancing on a makeshift dance floor that had been plopped down over the church lawn, I sort of meandered my way out into the parking lot amongst the pickup trucks and Buicks. I kept looking back over one shoulder, hoping the ol' gal would soon tire and Nee Nee and I would be on our way back home with some extra money to spend at Godfather's Pizza before catching a movie at the mall. In the parking lot, I saw a guy who looked like he could have played defensive line on a pretty good football team, sort of leaning on his truck, enjoying a beverage. The truck had those big magnetic business signs attached to the front doors: KCCE in bold letters, and then in italicized script below, *Kansas City Critter Extraction*.

Intrigued, I asked the guy, who looked to be about my age, about his extraction business.

Greg Cooper spent the next ten minutes, without even pausing for a breath of fresh air, educating me—*indoctrinating* me, almost—on the critter extraction business. I learned that in the old neighborhoods of Kansas City, where trees are abundant, there are legions of squirrels. Those squirrels can find their way into old homes, garages, businesses, and storage sheds, making a tremendous mess for the property owners to deal with. Now Greg Cooper was about six foot one and weighed at least two sixty—due to a pair of thighs that would make mature tree trunks jealous. There was no way he was the one crawling around in attics, basements, and crawl spaces to extricate these pesky squirrels (or sometimes pack rats, opossums, or even skunks, Greg told me) from these tight spaces.

The star of the KCCE company was his miniature terrier, Spanky.

"How does he get a squirrel?" I naively asked.

Greg was not shy with his answer. "O' Spanky just thrashes 'em. Here, I'll show ya."

Greg reached behind the bench seat of his truck and grabbed

what looked like a pair of dark socks. Greg went into the lineage of Spanky, one-eighth some kind of terrier and seven-eighths some other kind that I couldn't remember. He described his bone structure and how his ancestors had been bred to do this type of work for the past two centuries.

"That's why he's small enough to get in those tight spots and tough enough to take down any critter he's up against." He rolled the socks up into a ball and tossed the sock ball right to me.

"Spit on that and then go hide it . . . either behind another truck or over in those bushes there." He pointed to some trimmed hedges that lined the driveway up to the country church.

After giving Greg a strange look—I think I just kind of tilted my head in a "well okay" gesture—I spit into the sock ball and stuck it in the bushes about twenty yards away from Greg and his KCCE truck, then I came back to watch the dog perform.

That's when Greg and Spanky went to work. Greg carefully opened the animal carrier in the back of his truck. You could tell just by the way his kennel was secured in the truck and the expensive grade of material the carrier was made of that this pet was one well-cared-for animal.

Greg put Spanky, the seven-eighths Londonshire and one-eighth whatever terrier, on a leash, the kind that's more of a halter that wraps completely around the dog's body instead of just a typical collar with a hook on it, and walked him right up to me. I was looking down on this scrawny little dog that weighed maybe six pounds, tops. Then Greg said some command that sounded like "Soo-chen" or something like that. Greg told me, as if he was instructing an entire class down at the local animal shelter, "You don't use English words because you don't want someone to say something in a random conversation that will set your dog off to work." Greg said he used German commands, but he also admitted he wasn't sure it was

German because he called his grandma who spoke German as a child, but her mind wasn't very sharp anymore.

At the sound of Greg's command, Spanky sniffed my shoes for about five seconds.

"He's got your scent," Greg said and he slipped a treat to his coworker.

Then Greg unhitched his halter, and Spanky pranced in and out from underneath a few parked vehicles. Then, he made a beeline for those bushes, and in less than thirty seconds he had those socks in his mouth and was gnawing and tearing them to shreds!

For the next ten minutes, Greg explained how it took him only a week to train Spanky to "catch 'em and thrash 'em," and within another week, they were open for business, and Spanky was bringing in the "dead soldiers" as Greg liked to call them. I guess he meant the squirrels or skunks or whatever Spanky was able to get. He also told me how much he charged for his services, and at the time, I remember being quite impressed, but I can't remember the exact dollar figure. Nee Nee saw me from across the way and gave me a raised chin and a look that said, "We're leaving now." I gave her a smile and started thinking about pizza and a movie with my girl.

He gave me his card and said, "Ya never know."

That was the last time I talked to Greg Cooper.

———

"I'M GOING to take a different route home if it's okay with the two of you," Nee Nee said as she weaved her away around the edge of town and onto a paved county road.

The ol' gal nodded and let out with, "I hate the interstate freeway anyway." And we were off through the country.

"I like to look at the farms," Nee Nee said. "Some are neat as a pin, and others look like the last storm blew them to pieces and left debris everywhere." She started to say something else and then cut herself off by trying to tune the radio to a good station we could get out in rural America. Our favorite radio station had just gone country, and Nee Nee and I were in mourning about it.

"Nee Nee, you play Thursday afternoon, right?" I said, leaning up from the backseat. The ol' gal was about to drift to sleep. "At Bethany?"

"Yes, indeed. Doubles at one, Gawd, don't come for that. We will get killed. My match will be about three-ish, in Lindsborg."

"I'll be there," I said. "And then Friday, our big road trip out east." I started saying stuff with a fakey Boston accent (which Nadine didn't have, not even a *hint* of an accent), like, "Can't wait to pahk the cah near the hahbah," and "Beantown, here we come! Oh, I hope we can catch a Red Sox—excuse me, Saahx game."

I knew Bethany College had some chick from Europe who had beaten Nee Nee earlier in the year, so if they matched up again, it would be a tough match for Nee Nee. She was doing amazing for the Lady Coyotes, probably 11–2 or 12–3 in her singles on the year, but she never gave herself much credit when she did post a win. I figured a win over the Bethany chick from Denmark, or wherever, would be a lot different. If she could win this one, I think she'd bask in the Gatorade, so to speak.

"Where's that Bethany chick from, Nee Nee?" I asked as we glided over the county roads with the occasional stop sign for crossroads and small unincorporated towns.

"Why do you call her that?" came a voice from the front seat where I thought the ol' gal was sound asleep.

I didn't say anything, and then I heard it again, this time much more forcefully.

"Why do you call her that? If you loved her, you'd call her by her name." Her voice was pretty strong—and accusatory—for an old lady.

I didn't have much to say to that. I was going to stammer around and respond, but I could tell the ol' gal didn't give a dang about my response, so any reply would have fallen on a tightly closed mind, and anyway, I think she was right back to sleep.

I tried to change the mood and the details of the conversation as I gazed out at a small town beneath the shadow of its water tower. "That's a picturesque graveyard there, Nee Nee," I said with a gesture out the passenger side of the car.

"Actually," Nee Nee replied, "that's a cemetery. A graveyard is connected to church property."

"For real?" I questioned.

"Oh, yeah," Nadine went on. Her mood went from bored driver through the Kansas countryside to engaging informer. She explained how they had a huge debate about it in her Intro to Logic class, the best class she ever took, according to Nee Nee. Remember, this is before Google, so you'd have Dr. Perry leading her whole class down the sidewalk from Pioneer Hall to Carnegie Library to use reference books and try to come to an accepted truth.

"Dictionary, Schmictionary," Dr. Perry said. "Let's get to digging. Where did it originate? When was the first usage in our accepted lexicon? Did it spread across several languages? Are there conflicting solutions?" This was one of many reasons Nee Nee loved that class.

"Every day, we just search for validity . . . for the truth. You know, if all P is Q and some of S is P, how are Q and P related?" Nee Nee explained.

She really got into the nuts and bolts of thought puzzles like that. Nee Nee painted a good picture of it and how it ended up with Nadine and Dayton Loeffler, a cross-country runner from Canada, digging their heels in and refusing to surrender to the other. Just as Nee Nee was explaining how grateful she was that the proof was on her side, my mind was wandering back to my home life. Dad had a nickname for all of us—except my big sister, Marilyn.

Marilyn was two years older than me and born deaf. My parents worked danged hard to help Marilyn in every way they could. When she was a seventh grader, she went away to a boarding school for deaf kids in Omaha. She would still come home for holidays and summer, but it wasn't like having a full-time sibling. Any time I think of Marilyn, see a picture of her, or text or message with her, I always have the same feelings. Those feelings are that I didn't do hardly anything for her when we were growing up. I basically just ignored her. It was easy to do. She was quiet. Like, all-the-time quiet. She never asked me for anything. Other kids would complain about their big or little sibs being a pain in the neck, and I had absolutely nothing to add to the conversation. Anytime I would come across a deaf person out in public or even see one in a movie or television commercial, a wave of guilt came over me. I was never there for her, like a brother ought to be.

Anyway, Marilyn still lives in Nebraska. She married a guy who had a bike shop—he's deaf too. They closed the bike shop down because he makes a lot more money being a handyman. The guy can take anything apart, fix it, and put it back together. I can do the "take it apart" portion of that equation. For a while on his business cards, he had leopards, get it? He and Marilyn burst out laughing when they showed them to me.

"Oh, for real?" I signed, "You guys like Def Leppard?"

More laughter, and then Marilyn signed, "Who knows? We've never heard them!"

And then, later on, his business card's motto was, "I can fix anything, except your radio." She helps him and manages the business. They have a staff of about three or four fix-it men. They've got two grown kids and grandkids and will have a great-grandchild arriving soon. Marilyn is one of the happiest people I have ever known. Absolutely none of that happiness can be attributed to me. I did nothing to help her. So whenever I encountered anyone in the non-hearing world, my day was typically in for a wide swath of guilt and regret.

With basketball over, my afternoons were free for one entire week. Spring break would roll by, and then I'd start my new job at the shoe store in the mall. Why would I even remember such a detail? Because in four years of college, this was, by a landslide, the most free time I ever had. Basketball ate up every afternoon from the first day I stepped on campus until I checked in my practice jerseys the day after our last game four years later. We either had practice, weights, games, pick-up games, or "volunteer workouts" every weekday and nearly every weekend for four years. Those volunteer workouts? If you didn't show up, you just "volunteered" to run stadium steps at the football stadium for an hour the next day. Not complaining; it's just the schedule that college basketball players live. So, when it was over, I felt like I had all this free time on my hands.

I used my free time to make sure my car, a silver 1983 Volkswagen Golf, was in good shape for the drive to Boston that Nee Nee and I would start out for on Friday at about noon. I also went downtown to a jewelry store and purchased a necklace for Nee Nee. The nice lady at the jewelry store sold me on the fact that this necklace had both silver and gold elements, so "your lady" can wear it with almost anything. That "your lady" was a heckuva powerful selling line. As soon as she said that, my mind was made up.

I was going to give it to her after she beat the Euro chick from Bethany. If she didn't win that match, I'd wait until just the right time, maybe on the drive or when she showed me around her old high school stomping grounds. I borrowed some cash off one of my housemates, but I was proud of the purchase and looking forward to making a nice gift out of it for "my lady." I was rehearsing lines in my mind and trying to sound poetic. *Nee Nee, I hope that this small emblem is just the beginning of much more important jewelry I will give you in the future.* Oh, sheesh! Talk about awkward! *More important jewelry? Maybe more importanter or the most importantest jewelry ever!* It was clear why I got a C minus in public speaking class, and the C minus was a gift!

Thursday rolled around, I went to a couple of classes, lunch, and then out of force of habit, I guess, I found myself over in the gym shooting buckets and playing a few pickup basketball games. Time was starting to slip away, so I cut out and headed south the twenty miles to Lindsborg to watch some tennis. I would miss the doubles, but I just wanted to be there for Nee Nee—actually, I just wanted Nee Nee to see that I was there for her—there is, admittedly, a big difference.

A couple of things about college tennis matches.

1. Nobody goes to them.

2. They are quiet as a library.

When I got there, the four singles matches had already started. I headed over to Nee Nee's court and stood outside the fence behind the baseline. Some courts will have a few nice stadium seats or some random bleachers for onlookers. The tennis facility at Bethany had no seating, so some folks brought lawn chairs if they were planning on staying for the duration.

It's quiet. Nobody says a word. There is no referee or umpire. No ball boys are running around retrieving the balls for the players. There is no scoreboard. The players perform all these tasks; they are the referee, the ball boy, and the score-keeper. The sport has plenty of unwritten rules and bits of deco-rum. For instance, if you hit a ball that tips the top of the net and lands softly on your opponent's court, you win the point, but you are expected to apologize with a wave of the hand and an "Aw shucks, I'm sorry for your bad luck" facial gesture. In tennis etiquette, it is very bad form to make a call that slights your opponent. If it's close to the line and you're not sure, you make the call that favors your opponent. It is a huge no-no to accuse your opponent of making a bad call and, even worse, call for a judge or referee to settle a dispute. The players keep the score in their heads and will rarely call the score, and when they do, it's a soft, "My ad" or "Deuce."

Tennis is not the easiest of sports to score. A game is the first player to win four points by a margin of two. Apparently, scoring by ones or twos seemed illogical to the chaps that came up with the grand old game of tennis, so they numbered the points like this: fifteen, thirty, forty, game.

"Joel, think of it like the face of a clock. Your first point goes one-fourth of the way around the clock. That's fifteen. Your second point takes you to thirty," Nee Nee had tried to explain when we first started dating.

"Oh, okay," I said. "Fifteen, thirty, then why is it forty? What the heck happened to forty-five?"

"That's a long story, don't worry about it," Nee Nee said with a grin that made me want to scoot closer to her.

Anyway, if you lead 40–30 and win the next point, you have won the game. You need to win six games by a margin of two to win a set. You need to win two of three sets to win a match.

If the score of the game is 40–40, that is referred to as deuce. The winner of the next point now has an advantage, or "ad." You might hear, "My ad" or "ad in," which would mean you have the advantage, and if you win the next point, you get the game on your tally. Of course, if your opponent wins that point, it's back to deuce.

In fifteen minutes of play, you might hear, "Nice shot," or "three all." You've got to really pay attention to even try to figure out who is winning. So, I was watching the points, and all I was sure of was that this was a very even match-up. The Euro chick—it was the Netherlands—a Bethany girl told me, was uber-aggressive. She rushed the net at every opportunity, and everything she did just gave off an air of hustle, passion, and desire. Even the way she gave the ball a few bounces before she served was done with a burning intensity. She played every point like it was match point, with a few grunts and some self-cursing when she would hit a poor shot. In tennis, you play two games, then switch sides. Even in the way she pulled her hair back, replaced her visor, and examined her racket during the changeovers, she gave off an attitude of aggression.

Nee Nee played a more stoic, reserved style. You could never tell if she was winning or losing by her body language. She never looked like she was in a hurry. She stayed on the baseline for the most part and tried to use precision shots in the corners to defeat her opponent.

On one of the changeovers, the Bethany girl standing next to me called through the fence, "Racha, what's the score?"

The Bethany player answered, "She won first set. We are five-all in the second."

Finally! I had been there for about forty-five minutes and just found out the score.

Now, all I had to do was pay attention, and I would know what was going on. The good news was if Nee Nee could win this set, she would be getting a beautiful silver and gold neck-lace from me tonight, and well, this could turn out to be a *really* good day for the both of us.

The match was tight. The set went to a tiebreaker, and Racha won it. She was so excited I thought maybe the match was over but no, it was now even at one set apiece. They would play the third set to determine the winner. This set was extremely even, with games going into four or five deuce points. All the other matches were finished, so all the players and their various supporters gathered around to watch. The group standing near me made it clear that Bethany had won all seven matches. With all the people circling just this one court, it was starting to be a pretty good-sized crowd. Then, I noticed a lot of Bethany students were coming across campus. They were on their way to their cafeteria, which is right next to the tennis courts, so they streamed over to catch the buzz. Before long, there were about eighty people gathered around one court, watching two girls in a battle of will and skill.

Their crowd was becoming more and more engaged with the action on the court. I glanced down to the other end, and I saw why. The point guard from their basketball team, a cocky little shit named Dennison, had decided to take on the role of head cheerleader. After each point Nee Nee lost, he was getting them riled up. If Nee Nee won the point, it was silence. One game, while Nee Nee was serving, he had the crowd doing the wave. The Bethany tennis coach walked over to the kids and told them they couldn't do that during play. It calmed them, but only a little.

Nee Nee didn't seem to be bothered by the crowd, but I did notice her pace picking up. She wasn't her deliberate self. She was hurrying to pick up balls and hurrying herself to serve. She was letting Euro chick dictate the pace of play. And then, at five-all in the third set, with Nee Nee serving, I thought I detected a change in her that bothered me something awful.

Nee Nee gave the game away.

She double-faulted twice . . . it almost looked like it was on purpose. The crowd was going nuts. Dennison had them chanting, "Clean sweep! Clean sweep!" and "Eight in a row! Eight in a row!" and maybe some other stuff I didn't even understand, but it was all getting very annoying.

Euro chick served, leading 6–5, and Nee Nee kept it even for a while. Then, at the second deuce point, Nee Nee let a shot go that maybe she thought was going to sail wide, but it was in by a foot.

What was she doing? Why was she giving in like that? This couldn't be Nee Nee. She was always the one who stood strong and unwavering. I was biting my cheek in an anger that had no possible outlet. Usually, there's a ref to yell at if you are frustrated at a sporting event. Or you can call out encouragement for your team. Here I was, surrounded by the enemy, and my team seemed to be giving the game away!

On match point, Nee Nee's return hit smack in the middle of the net, and the match was over. The Bethany kids all rushed onto the court to greet their winner while Nee Nee quickly grabbed her bag, extra racket, and water bottle and walked off after a quick handshake and smile at the net.

The weird part, for me, was that I thought I detected a wry little smile on Nee Nee's lips as she walked off with her gear. She didn't look disappointed or angry. Those emotions crawl all over my face after a loss, especially a narrow loss when I felt I had a chance to win. She looked like she had just checked something off her list. Groceries, done. Vacuum out the car, done. Lose a tight, three-set match in front of a huge crowd (for tennis), done. She was looking ahead as she walked off that court like she was just going through her day. It startled me. I didn't really know what to say. I was going to go over and talk to her, but she didn't look left or right, even though she knew I was directly to her left. She just got into the team van, and they whooshed their way out of the parking lot and headed back to Kansas Wesleyan.

Later that night, I went over to where Nee Nee and the old lady lived. I hopped up the porch steps to the well-kept bungalow on Highland Street and saw Nadine talking with a friend of hers (I called her Indira because she was from India). Nee Nee was giving Indira instructions about the house and caring for the ol' gal.

"Let's leave super early," Nee Nee said before I could even say hello.

"I thought you had a nine o'clock?" I said, knowing Nee Nee never missed classes.

"I'm not going," she said. "There won't be anybody there."

"Okay, well, I will have Silver all gassed up and ready to go."

I kind of moved close to give her a little cheek-kiss slash pat on the shoulder. She wasn't having it in front of her friend.

"See ya bright and early, Joel." Then, turning fully away from me and toward her friend, "I better show you this freezer out in the garage. It's on its last legs . . ."

———

THAT NIGHT, I finished packing up for our big spring break trip to Boston. I'd never been further east than St. Louis with my family one time when I was about ten to see the arch and a Cardinals baseball game. I was excited to see the rest of the country, and spending the week with Nee Nee was going to be a lot better than that trip to St. Louis with Mom, Dad, Marilyn, and a cousin we hauled along with us who was super whiney and such a picky eater he got to dictate all our plans. I chuckled out loud when I remembered halfway through that trip the nickname my dad gave that little cousin. He was such a picky eater, he perused an entire restaurant menu and proclaimed, "They don't have anything I like."

So, Dad said, "You can eat your own boogers then."

And little cousin Thad became "Boogers" just like that.

CHAPTER THREE
JOE MILLER

Joe had made a living as a contractor. He hired day laborers and was masterful at getting a lot of work out of them for a small wage. He bid low; he paid low. He didn't buy trusted, quality construction materials when shoddy, second-rate materials—that would be covered up or masked in some way that a customer would never know—could finish the job. Joe paid his workers in cash, took on jobs for cash, and claimed about a tenth of what he actually took in every year to good, old Uncle Sam, as Joe liked to tell everyone. And tell everyone he did. He bragged about how anyone who was stupid enough to pay taxes in this day and age to the dishonest government we suffered under just deserved to have his money go to thousand-dollar coffee pots in the Army and some space shuttle that blew up in the sky.

Joe loved to hunt and fish just south of his home in Hutchinson, Kansas. He'd formed enough friendships to have a nice pick of ponds to pull bass out of and wooded land to bring down a white-tailed deer each December. Joe had been married twice, with two kids from each wife. "Keep the score even, ya know," he would say while having a beer at his favorite tavern in South Hutchinson.

The only thing Joe loved to brag about more than how he withheld money from the government was his gun collection. He had quite a large stockpile of weapons ranging from the biggest old rifles of various brands to the smallest derringer pistols you could imagine. His prized possessions were a pair of matching Samuel Colt .38 caliber pistols he had "finagled an old boy from Texas out of." He said he did some work for the Texan one winter and this particular Texan was a little short on cash. While on that job, Joe had noticed the six shooters in a display case and came home with them the next day. According to Joe's two boys, every time Joe told the story, it was a little different. The value of the guns, the year they were made, the previous owners, the famous gunfight they'd been used in—all these sundry details would be adjusted depending on the audience. The accounts were sometimes eye-rollingly hard to believe. They agreed, though, that each time he spoke about the two Colt pistols, anyone within a city block could tell they were his prized possessions, and he would never part with them.

About four nights a week—"Friday's too busy around here, people poking into my business"—Joe would have a basket of onion rings and a few draft beers at his favorite tavern, House of Suds.

"Your daughter was in here about an hour ago, Joe, and she was loaded for bear," the bartender said. "She said you skipped your doctor's appointment."

"Yeah, I might have forgot." Joe shrugged and sipped his beer.

"She said if she finds out you were at that gun auction in Lyons, you will be in some serious hot water," the bartender warned.

"Dang that girl. How did she find out about that?"

"They're smart these days. She looked ready to raise a knot on the side of your head."

"All right, I'll be on the lookout for her. Gimme a basket of your onion rings, Robert," Joe said.

"Sure enough," and the bartender was off to the fryer.

CHAPTER FOUR
SPRING BREAK

T he drive to Boston with Nee Nee dragged on for three reasons.

1. It's about 1,600 miles from the middle of Kansas to Boston, Massachusetts.
2. The speed limit in 1987 was 55 mph, which turned long trips into prolonged torture by car seat.
3. I had this aching need to talk to Nee Nee about that match she gave away to the European chick, but it's pretty hard to tell someone they stink at a sport they are truly very good at.

I decided the necklace and any talk about the tennis match could wait a few days. We were here to have a good time and see the sights. We were also going to make a little money because Nadine had arranged a job for us. We were going to move a bunch of boxes and file cabinets for a neighbor who I was assured would pay us handsomely for our labor. Nee Nee always had a better bank account than mine due to the generous ol' gal she assisted, but we could definitely use the cash for the trip back home.

We nearly made it to Dayton, Ohio, on day one and found a super cheap roadside motel on the outskirts of the city. It was a short night in Ohio, and the all-day drive on Saturday brought us into Boston around 11 p.m. when we pulled into Nee Nee's parent's driveway. It was a small, red brick home—any movie director would choose it for a modest northeastern family home —with probably two bedrooms on the first floor and two small bedrooms upstairs. The houses were jammed together tight in this neighborhood, and even my small Volkswagen was a challenge to park on the narrow, crowded street.

The house was quiet as Nadine's folks were asleep. She pointed me to a bedroom upstairs that had a bare mattress with clean sheets folded on the foot of the bed. She warmly held me and said, "Thank you for helping me get here. I couldn't have done this trip by myself."

I said, "I love you, Nee—I mean, Nadine. I'm glad to be here with you." We kissed for a few minutes, which felt amazing because the night before in Ohio, we both just went right to sleep. I was instantly liking Boston much more than Ohio! Then, Nee Nee went downstairs to her old room, and I quickly went to sleep.

The next morning, I woke up, made the bed, and went down the steps to a very quiet main floor. The kitchen and living room were small but tidy, and the walls were covered with crosses, crucifixes, and family photos.

Nee Nee had just showered and said, "My parents left early for Mass. They will be gone all day visiting family and doing who knows what at the church."

"The Red Sox have a day game on Wednesday," I said, "and we are supposed to work for your neighbor tomorrow and Tuesday, right?"

Nadine nodded.

"So . . . today, you could just show me around, you know, the beach, the Paul Revere stuff, etcetera," I suggested.

"That's the plan." Nee Nee pointed to a basket on the kitchen counter. She had made up a nice picnic lunch for us and thrown in some towels and sun lotion. We enjoyed the day like we were making a commercial for the Massachusetts Bureau of Tourism: Boston Common, Old North Church, Quincy Market. For a Kansas boy, it was exhilarating. We got home well after dark, about ten-ish, but her parents weren't back yet. We went to our separate beds at about eleven, and then I heard them quietly come home just a few minutes later.

Monday morning, first thing, is when the shit hit the fan!

I came downstairs and saw Nee Nee sitting at the kitchen table. Mrs. Blass was standing at the sink. She was a much shorter woman than her daughter. They both had dark eyes and similar cheek and chin structures. Yes, I could see it. Nadine resembled her mother quite a bit, except for the expression in the lines on Mrs. Blass's face. Those were lines of indignation. Those were lines of accusation.

I was about to say good morning, and it looked as if Nee Nee was about to introduce me.

But Mrs. Blass beat us to the punch, and she left no doubt as to her sentiments about Nee Nee and me.

"So, is this the guy you spent all day yesterday fucking in my house?"

I was stunned into silence and a statuesque standstill.

Nee Nee looked down at her folded hands on the kitchen table.

"Remember Doug Carlson from high school? You sucked his dick in this very kitchen, didn't you, Nadine? And that oldest Newton boy." Mrs. Blass's eyes narrowed. " I bet you fucked him in my bed! My very own bed. I bet you fucked him until he couldn't walk straight! Probably while your father and I were at Mass!"

Mr. Blass quietly walked in from the front room, poured some freshly made coffee into a stainless-steel thermos, screwed the lid back on tightly, said, "I'll be home about five," walked out the side door, backed his truck down the narrow, steep driveway, and took off.

Nee Nee calmly said, "Mom, we are going to help the Fraziers today. Come on, Joel," and we quickly left.

There were about four similar outbreaks during our stay. Only once more was sexual talk involved, thank goodness. The other outbursts centered on poor performance in school: "Three B's your senior year after all A's . . . that's what partying gets you, Nadine Blass." Tennis was also the feature of one outburst: "If you would have gone to that summer camp, you'd be playing at U Mass instead of out there in the sticks. And you wouldn't be dragging this loafer around with you," she jerked a thumb my way. "Probably be engaged to a pre-med or an engineer by now. Do you know what an engineer makes these days, Nadine? You could have been set for life!"

Nadine just maintained her calm throughout the entire week. At least until I screwed that up near St. Louis on the drive home.

CHAPTER FIVE
ROADKILL

Just thinking about luck. If there is good luck, and I fully believe in that, I guess you've got to admit that there is bad luck. People get cancer or any number of diseases: I call that bad luck. But I suppose some chemist or DNA expert would say, "That is just science. There was no luck involved. The living cells all interact with one another and produce a totally predictable result. There is no luck involved, good or bad."

I'm sorry, but I'm digging my heels in on this one. You might have your three degrees from Johns Hopkins Medical Hoo Haw, but I will always believe there is good luck and bad.

One time, I was driving across western Nebraska all by myself. A good buddy of mine, who went to high school with me, got a football scholarship to play linebacker at Chadron State College, clear up in the northwestern corner of Nebraska. That's the top left-hand corner on a map for you geography whizzes. It was a long and lonely drive that provided me with a lot of time to think at 59 mph. A *lot* of time.

Just about any time I had that much time to think, my mind would quickly become bored with thoughts of basketball or school, and then those pesky neurons and axons and dendrites and all those brain cells would work in unison to dredge up Nee Nee. Well, thoughts of Nee Nee anyway.

Our first break-up lasted only a couple of weeks. I blame the lasagna.

Nee Nee and I had been together for maybe a month. Things were great. I had an attractive girl waiting for me in the foyer after a basketball game. Allen Wagner might have had eighteen and eleven against Bethel College, but I had Nee Nee standing there in a nice peacoat and a fashionable pair of boots, peering through the line of boys leaving a locker room, their happiness dependent on the final score of a small college basketball game. All of the guys on the team noticed Nee Nee, and some of the guys on the team even called her "Boots" because she seemed to have several pairs. What it pointed out to me was that she looked dang good in those boots, so what did I care?

A locker room is the most honest place on Earth. If you have weird feet, moles on your back, or, yeah, even something weird about your man plumbing, it's going to be called out and talked about in the locker room. The only line that won't be crossed is to call someone's girl ugly. If they are talking about her, it means they are jealous. So, the more they talked about Boots, the more I was okay with it.

Just about any college dude would give up a good dorm room or even their mini fridge to have someone like Nee Nee to walk with to Kwik Shop or Hardees late at night for a snack after studying. Well, studying for her. For me, it was after card games or dice baseball games in the dormitory lobby.

The dang lasagna. It was a Friday night during the basketball season of my junior year, and Nee Nee invited me over to her place for a nice handmade meal. Easy choice. Eat in the college cafeteria with a bunch of sweaty guys after practice, or get cleaned up and go over to my lady's house and dine on something wonderful. There is more to it than that, but basically, would you rather eat or dine? A feed trough versus an enchanting dinner. I think you get my point.

Nee Nee made a wonderful meal. A fresh garden salad, toasted garlic bread, a bottle of cheap wine, and the star of the show: her lasagna.

"This lasagna tastes a little funny," I said.

That was what I said. I said those words. I uttered probably a hundred other sentences that night before I blurted that unwise assessment of Nee Nee's lasagna. I told her about basketball practice that evening. I told her some stories that I thought were funny and entertaining. I also did an imitation of an old professor going through roll call and mispronouncing the same names every Monday, Wednesday, and Friday. I made sure she knew we played a home game the following evening at Muir Gym, and I could just envision her watching from about four or five rows up with some of her girlfriends who were also in the education department. I could see her waiting for me as I exited the locker room. If we won, Coach B's talks were usually under five minutes. A loss could bump the post-game talk past ten minutes, an interminable amount of time when you know exactly what is going to be said and the way it's going to be said.

Even after a loss, the vision of Nee Nee would ease the irritation of Coach B's monologue. Which boots would she wear, and if only Coach put me on Dewberry, their best rebounder, so I could prove once and for all that I had more value to the team than Coach B realized.

"Tastes funny?" she asked.

As soon as she said "funny," I realized I had picked the absolute stupidest adjective in Webster's unabridged that I could have possibly uttered.

Maybe I would try silence.

"Funny, Joel? What did you find *funny* about it?" she demanded.

"I just mean different. Your seasoning is really good," I offered.

Now, the silence came from her.

"I think I'm just used to my mom's. It's a Kansas lasagna, I guess. And your Boston lasagna caught me by surprise. I like it." I was rambling, but I couldn't stop. "I think my mom used beef in her lasagna . . . cuz it's Kansas and, well, it's beef country. Is that sausage in yours? Nadine?"

She gave me a look like I had just told Picasso I preferred fingerpainting to his work.

Still with the silence.

"Nee Nee, let me help you clean up, and we'll play a game of Yahtzee or watch MASH," I suggested hopefully.

She walked over to her phone on the wall and called a friend.

"Hey, Anne, are you guys still going to Manhattan tomorrow night? Save me a seat. Sounds like a blast." She hung up and walked out of the room.

Tomorrow? We had a home game tomorrow, and she knew it.

I didn't say one word about that salad, and it was good. I didn't compliment the garlic bread, lightly toasted, I might add, and it was fantastic. I didn't thank her or tease her about the wine; it was cheap, and it hit the spot.

Nope. I had to say her lasagna tasted funny.

She wasn't there the following night after the game. I came out of the locker room and there was no Nee Nee. No fashionably dressed, intelligent woman with boots to kill waiting for me. No cozy walk across campus. No . . . well, I don't need to spell it out for you any further.

That lonely highway on the way to Chadron State College provided me with way too much time to think.

Once it got dark, it was so remote out there that you couldn't see a light, a power pole, or any sign of human civilization except the nice, smooth highway I was driving on. I went forty or fifty miles without dimming my headlights. I was truly alone on US Highway 385. Then I saw a dead animal, pretty sure it was a raccoon, on the side of the road. It had been splattered by a fast-moving vehicle.

In the thousands and thousands of acres that my eyes had scanned in the past thirty minutes, I had not seen one vehicle, so it stands to reason there was very, very little traffic on this road. Yet, there was a dead raccoon who picked one of the very few times he could not safely cross Highway 385. He, or she, literally had thousands of acres, thousands of square miles where the little critter could have lived out a perfectly happy life.

That's bad luck for that raccoon. I can't call it anything else. Bad luck.

My buddy got to play the whole game and made a bunch of tackles. After seeing the home team win, the field was full of students, fans, and family members huddled around their favorite Myrmidons of the gridiron. I placed my palms together like I was going to dive into a swimming pool and tried to make my way through a throng of happy football fans. I found my friend wearing his untucked number 58 jersey. He was covered in grass, mud, sweat, and a huge grin.

"Dang, you didn't tell me you'd be starting," I said. "Great game."

"I didn't even know. I've only been getting two or three plays a game, but last night, our starting inside linebacker broke his wrist in the dorm. He was doing laundry and slipped on a puddle. Just bad luck—for him."

The lasagna remark, I guess, quickly faded away for Nee Nee because, after a few days, she found me playing ping-pong in the student center and said, "Hey Joel, can you help me move some furniture around upstairs for my landlady?"

I knew we were made up when I saw the furniture in question was not at all heavy. Nee Nee could have easily arranged the room alone. We then went downstairs, and I secretly spent the night in the basement with Nee Nee.

The splattered raccoon and the puddle-prone linebacker—bad luck.

Me getting away with a stupid judgment of pasta—good luck. Very good luck.

CHAPTER SIX
TOTALLY FORKED

You've heard the expression "the elephant in the room" used to describe that human situation when everyone in the room knows there is a certain topic that nobody in the room wants to address. The topic is the elephant, and no matter how large or stinky or imposing that elephant appears, no one wants to be the first to say, "Hey, we've got a pachyderm problem in this four-walled cubicle."

Our trip back to Kansas from Boston—that's 1,600 miles—included three elephants squeezed into my Volkswagen Golf. I've never calculated the square footage of a Volkswagen before, but it fills up quite quickly when three elephants try to cram their way inside.

Three elephants? Yes, three that I could think of right off the top of my head.

1. Nee Nee's mom, slash childhood, slash what in the heck was that we just witnessed?
2. The tennis match was still bugging me! Why did she let that Euro chick get away with an easy win after battling her for two hours so strenuously? It was like Sir Edmund Hillary getting to within a few hundred

feet of the top of Mount Everest, turning around, and saying, "Aw, what the heck, I'm done."

3. What about us? Nee Nee and me, what were we? Was this a thing that was going on into the future? What did our future entail? I was lining up a part-time job at a shoe store, and Nee Nee had interviews scheduled to be a middle school teacher.

So, as the miles went by, the silence was digging into my soul, and I could feel a wedge separating Nee Nee and me that was about to split my Volkswagen with a metaphorical fork in the road. As we were traveling west on I-70, that fork in the road was beginning to feel like I was in Texas and Nee Nee was in North Dakota. Unlike Emerson or Thoreau, or whoever it was that wrote that poem, I was coming to a fork in the road, and I wanted to take the one that would include Nee Nee going with me, but I was getting signals that were emanating in strong, silent waves that Nee Nee might want to choose whichever fork in the road I didn't choose.

Seeing the arch in St. Louis must have sent some subliminal message to me that said, "Gee, Joel, now would be a good time for you to say something that will totally change the trajectory of your life. Go ahead, let it rip!"

"Hey, Nadine," I started out, and already, my voice was showing a weak, almost trembling quality, so I knew this wasn't going to turn out so great. "I wanted to ask you about the tennis match."

"Yeah," Nee Nee said. "Two more regular season meets, and then we have regionals." Her tone was without timbre or emotion. She could have been the voice at a drive-thru fast food saying, "Pull up to the next window."

"No." I decided to go ahead and deal with elephant number two. "The Bethany match. It looked like you . . ."

I kind of stalled and thought maybe she would interrupt with a, "What, I should have just taken a little pace off my serve or tried to rush the net a little?" But she just left me hanging on the tusk of the elephant. Hanging by one hand . . . one finger . . . way out on the edge of that tusk.

"Nee, it was almost like you . . . you just gave it to her at the end."

Still, silence from the other seat in the VW.

"And then when the match ended . . . you just kind of grinned," I stated.

I don't know how big the counties are in Missouri, but for the next four counties, Nee Nee didn't stop. She unloaded on me with the intensity of the engines on the Apollo rocket that took Neil Armstrong to the moon.

"Oh, you are fucking kidding me right now, Joel Howard! I grinned? I *grinned*? Oh, I didn't have shit all over my face with flaming red cheeks and cussing about a referee or blaming the coach for not putting me on the guy who got all the rebounds like you after every loss of the last two years? And that's a lot of fucking losses! Okay, Joel, since you asked—or should I say, since you whined—I will let you in on a little secret. I now know how to beat her. It didn't mean shit who won the other night. If I beat her at regionals, I go to nationals in Phoenix. That's been my goal for four years. You wouldn't know that. You see, I *would* know that your goal at the beginning of your year was to start, be All-Conference, or at least honorable mention, and finish in the top three teams of the conference. Oops. Zero for three on those lofty goals, Joel Howard! Oh well, that's the way the ball bounces.

"Oh, back to my grinning. Was I grinning? Or was I smiling? Or was it a smirk? I know what it was! It was a full-on giggle. You know why? Because the next time I play her, I am going to destroy her. And I am going to enjoy it. I am going to beat her, and I know *exactly* how I am going to do it. I only needed to find the key. But finding the key and then exposing that key to her coach—cuz they have a real fucking tennis coach, and we have a fucking chauffeur—if her coach saw that I found a path, he would work with her on it. He'd prepare her. He'd have her ready. So, I didn't expose the key to him, and I'm not telling anyone else either, so don't ask, not that you care.

"Is that what you've been so uptight about on this trip? Sheesh, Joel, you've used your brilliant tennis analyst mind to deduce I tanked a match on purpose? What? I'm not made from the mentally tough mold that is worthy to date or go into the future with *the* Joel Howard. I might have flaws that would hold *Joel* back? Character flaws? Glitches in the old DNA? You visit my family one time, and now you see the whole picture, eh?

"Oh, I bet you've had a helluva lot of fun with some Freudian-level shit thinking about me and my background. Okay, yes, my parents are a trainwreck. Yep, well, that's what happens when Dad goes through life rip-roaring drunk every day for the last ten years, and Mom wants everyone in the city to think she is the best Catholic, the best seamstress, the best mom, the best room mother—oh, I've got about seven stories each to back up those claims."

I sadly have to admit that when Nee Nee mentioned her dad going through life drunk every day—well, in my crappy mind, all I could think of was, *Dang, how did he back that truck and trailer down that narrow driveway? I mean, he had like three inches between his truck and the wall of the house and then he turned that thing on a dime when he got to the street. It was like a clinic on how to back a truck and trailer. I wish I had it on video.*

"I've been to your hometown a few times. I saw that meal your mom served us at Easter last year. The nice China, the linens. Your vanilla childhood all spilled out in front of me. What were there, *fifty* pictures of you playing sports scattered around the place? Those honor roll clippings from middle school and high school on the side of the refrigerator are beginning to yellow, but hey, when the folks love their kid, they tend to leave stuff like that lying around to prove it.

"'Oh, Miss Kimball is old, but she is perceptive.' 'If you loved her, you'd call her by her name.' Jesus jumping Christ, Joel. I was *grinning*. G-W-L: grinning while losing. What a crime.

"Oh, and back to my mom. She was wrong about one thing: I never sucked Doug Carlson's dick in her kitchen or anywhere. I never even saw his dick. Now, Tyler Newton, she was right about that one. I fucked that guy in every room of our house and his. *And* both of our cars.

"Oops, I almost forgot. The lasagna! That funny-tasting stuff? It's called ricotta and grated parmesan, Joel. Grated. *Fresh.* Not that crappy powdered kind you Kansans shake on a pizza like a can of Comet into a rusty kitchen sink. Better put some shake cheese on my *Eye-talian* food," she mockingly said.

Well, I guess I brought up the first elephant, but Nadine was certainly going through a herd of elephants at light speed. Is it a herd of elephants? A pack? A cluster? They were trampling me to shreds, and the miles could not pass by quickly enough.

That necklace was so far buried in my bag that I may as well have been thinking about shipping it to my sister for a Christmas present. At that point in my life, I just wasn't mature enough to understand that Nee Nee had just unloaded a lifetime of baggage—no, that's too trivial—a lifetime of emotion, feelings, and soul, and she needed support and reassurance. In fact, my immaturity had me thinking, *Where do I go from here? I can't help it if my parents are normal. I guess this Tyler Newton guy must have just been the greatest . . .*

It only took Nee Nee about five more miles to see that I didn't have the emotional depth or skill to empathize. Even an argument would have validated her in some way. I just left it hanging. I basically gave her the same attention I would give a person on the corner holding a cardboard sign that says Money

Please. Just walk on by, maybe a little shucks-what-a-tough-life head tilt.

With only a few miles left, I started to think I should at least defend Mom, but nope, not a word. When we pulled into the drive at the ol' gal's house, I helped Nee Nee take a bag or two up to the porch.

"Nee Nee," I said, just kind of looking at my shoes, "I hope you get some sleep, and maybe let's get lunch together on Monday after your eleven o'clock."

Just for the record, I do not and have never pronounced it *Eye-talian.*

Standing on Miss Kimball's porch and staring at a closed door felt like the words "The End" flashing on the screen of a movie. A movie you didn't want to end, in a theater you didn't want to leave.

CHAPTER SEVEN
CAREER OPPORTUNITIES

C lasses, finals, and a spring formal without Nee Nee and graduation buzzed right on by. There I was, a guy with a business degree without a business. I did complete a short internship with an independent insurance agent that actually went pretty well. "Selling car insurance is a sure winner," that was my dad's advice. "Everyone's gotta have it."

The job at the shoe store wasn't the worst existence. Manager David was pretty good to me. He taught me a lot about inventories, ordering, accuracy, hiring, scheduling, and forecasts. He explained the hierarchy in retail: franchise stores, company stores, regional managers—the "oh shit guy," David called them. "Cuz if a regional manager walks in your back door unannounced, you're going to say, 'Oh, shit.'"

He broke it down with tremendous clarity. He gave great examples of stores he'd worked in and the managerial strategies he had seen be very successful. He was especially glad to share some strategies that were miserable failures.

I can easily say he was a better business teacher than some of the instructors I had in college. He quickly gave me a raise and more hours. He made me an assistant manager, which really didn't mean much. I had a key to the back door and one to that big metal gate that slid across the front of the store. I counted the drawer at the end of the day, made a deposit slip in triplicate with two slips of carbon paper, and walked the deposit about fifty yards over to the bank inside the mall a few minutes after closing time. The night deposit slot was between the inner and outer mall doors. Some of the managers would sneak a quick smoke in if it was a cold night. We would usually talk sports. Jayhawks and Wildcats results will hold the interest of most Kansans. Some of the managers would talk numbers: "Man, we crushed our forecast today," or "We are way down for the week, I hope we catch up on Saturday." I was getting good at timing my deposit at the same time that a few of the more "desirable" managers would drop their deposits. I tried to time it to coincide with an attractive gal who managed a chic boutique, and once in a while, a couple of the perfume girls from Dillard's would walk on down to drop off deposit bags. I was a little on the shy side and didn't say much at first, but I was getting a little flirtier as the summer stretched on.

Anytime I called my folks or made a quick visit to their house, my dad would mention I was working a job that any high school graduate could be doing. "It sure is a good thing you paid all that money to that college so you could work at a shoe store."

My dad's snarky comments would leap into my mind when I was making the night deposit at the same time a high school kid from one of the other mall stores was sent to make their deposit. One particular night, a girl, who was probably seventeen or eighteen but looked all of about fourteen years old, came bopping down to the bank's night deposit. "Super Glue" was her earned nickname. She could get her bangs to stick straight up into the air, as was the fashion of the day, and the way they defied gravity, I guess I granted that nickname on the basis of my determination that no hair spray could pull that off. The slot for night deposits was almost identical to the book drop at your average city library. You'd pull down on a stainless-steel handle, the door would slant open, and you dropped your deposit bag or bags down the chute. At the library, you can hear your book hit the stack of books or the floor below. At the bank, the deposit bags pile up inside a cardboard or metal box, and the bank staff works the bags before the bank opens the next morning. You can stop in any time the following day to pick up your bags, receipts, and a change order, if you requested one.

Super Glue had come from the cookie company or something, and when she opened the slot and dropped her cash bag right in front of me, I heard her exclaim, "Oh, crap, my bracelet!" Her jewelry had slipped right off her wrist and fallen down the chute into the bank.

I tried to comfort her a little, "Don't worry. They'll hold onto it for you, and you can pick it up tomorrow any time after they open. They're real nice ladies who work there."

She was convinced she could reach through the slot and retrieve the bracelet, even though this was not physically possible. I was impressed that Super Glue got her skinny, little wrist and arm stuck into that slot almost up to her elbow.

I repeated my message about the bank being open in the morning and that they would have it for her, and she responded with, "Oh well. It was just a crappy little cheap thing anyway."

I could watch from my counter and look down the way to time my walk to the bank to meet up with the boutique manager. I definitely wanted to get to know her a little better. I even had a nickname for her already: Titleist. Like the golf balls, cuz of her dimples.

All in all, I felt like the mall employees, especially the managers, had good camaraderie. None of us were getting rich in the world of retail, but it made working there a positive experience overall. I've heard plenty of stories about people having to work with fellow staff that they despise. I felt fortunate how well we all got along. For instance, I was getting a slice at

Sbarro, America's mall pizzeria, one time, and the manager and I were just chatting. He was just a couple of years older than me, so we had a pretty good "chatting relationship," I would say. Brad Phillips said he was a single guy from Oklahoma, and as soon as one of the Sbarro franchises down there needed a new manager, he was "blowing this popsicle stand" in his Oklahoma twang. He wanted to get back to his home state and manage a pizza place there. He said he had to make a run down to their store in Hutchinson and deliver a few items they were running low on, small paper cups and carry-out boxes.

"We help each other out like that. One time, my truck forgot to unload the cheese I ordered. Pretty hard to make pizza all week without cheese. The customers tend to catch on," Brad laughed.

"Anyway, you need anything from your Hutch store?" he asked.

"I don't, but since you're heading that way, let me call Lane down there. He may need something," I said.

Sure enough, our Hutchinson store, about fifty-some miles to the south of Salina, was out of a very popular men's walking shoe that was really flying off the shelf. Our Salina store had plenty, so I sent a dozen pairs that way. He'd bring me back replacements when he got his next order.

"Thanks, Brad," I said. "Next time your truck messes you over, make sure you let me know, and I'll help you out."

"No problem," Brad said as he took off his apron and then walked with me down the mall corridor to the shoe store to get a dozen pairs of the tan "Agile Man" men's walking shoes.

While there were many positive aspects of my shoe store job, one fact remained, I still searched the want-ads in the newspaper every day for a different job.

My typical summer days consisted of waking up in our rented house with different "guests" sleeping on couches or sleeping bags. Guys we had gone to college with a year or so ago would stop by for a few days to hang out with friends, or they would be in between jobs or looking for an apartment. Sometimes, guys I barely knew would spend the night after being out a little too late and drinking a little too much. In 1987, the job market was lousy, which made me glad to have a job at all. Still, I continued mailing job applications to various businesses all over Central Kansas.

One college friend who had moved in for the summer and was helping to pay bills was a guy who had been on the baseball team at Kansas Wesleyan. Toby was coaching a team of fourteen- and fifteen-year-old boys in the local Babe Ruth Baseball League. The parents of the boys had all chipped in a little money to pay Toby, but he still needed to find a day job or at least something to get him through the summer before he returned to Wesleyan for his senior year of school and baseball. I told Toby we didn't have any openings at the shoe store, but maybe the manager at the pizza place would hire him.

"Manager's name is Brad," I told Toby. "Just come to the mall with me today, and I will introduce you guys. I bet he could use you at least part-time. He's a good guy."

I didn't begin my shift that day until 1 p.m., so Toby and I kind of meandered through the mall, just window shopping and chatting. One of the dads from the Babe Ruth team that Toby was coaching saw us and came right up to Toby.

"My kid is having a lot of fun this summer," baseball dad said. "He really likes practices the way you run them."

"Well, thanks," Toby said. "He is doing great. He's got a nice arm."

Then, baseball dad added, "And I like the way you coach. If the pitcher starts walking guys, you get him out of there. You give somebody else a chance. I mean, it makes sense."

Toby just grinned, and we kind of walked on. We headed down to the food court, and the aroma of a hot dog was enticing me, but I thought we better patronize Brad's pizza stand, so I bought a couple of slices, and then when I could get the manager's attention, I waved him over.

"Hey, Brad, this is Toby. Toby, Brad. Toby is a college friend of mine and is looking for some part-time work if you could use him this summer."

After about a five-minute conversation, Toby left with a paper job application in hand.

"Did he say he'd hire you?" I asked.

"I think so," Toby said. "That guy is a little on the twisted side."

"Really? Like how?"

"Five percent of that conversation was about me getting a job there, and the other 95 percent was about him and all the women in this mall that want him, or so he claims." We approached the mall doors, and an older gentleman was holding the door for us.

"O . . . kay," I said hesitantly, "not your typical job interview."

We approached the outer doors of the mall, and a middle-aged gentleman held the door for us. Just as I was saying, "Thank you, sir," the door-holder said, "Hey, Coach. Good to see you," directed at Toby.

We stopped, and this was baseball dad number two. He was also impressed with the way the boys were responding to Toby's coaching and heaped some high praise on my college buddy. He ended the conversation with the comment I remember the most.

"You know what I've noticed?" baseball dad number two said. "When a pitcher gets in a little trouble, you don't just yank him out of there right away. You give him a chance to wriggle off the hook. Gives the kids confidence. I like that."

Toby and I walked out the doors and shared a look with each other, then a good laugh.

It really made me think about coaching. Perspectives can sure be different. Here were two dads with their boys playing in the same games for the same coach, and they were taking away totally different snapshots from the experience.

It got me thinking about my experiences with Coach B and the different roles that kids and coaches play within the structure of a team. As a bench guy, I had a lot of jobs that the average basketball fan would have no idea about. Fans might think your number one priority is to be ready to be called on to come off the bench and lead your team to a rousing victory.

Yeah. If you're making a Disney movie. Your main job as a bench guy is to stay out of the way. That's right, *stay out of the way*. Stay out of the way of the starters when they come over for a time-out. Stay the heck out of the way of the head coach when he is pacing around or looking for water or a legal pad or a marker. Stay out of the way of the manager. They have to get the water and the towels and stuff delivered. So yeah, just stay out of the way.

And nod. Nod your gosh darned head a lot. If a coach is talking, you get to nodding. Oh, and high fives. You will need to give every player a high five when they come out of the game. If they miss eight shots in a row, you still give them a high five. If their guy is open all night, that's not your worry, you give him a high five. Also acceptable are low fives or a five on the side. If you are white and the guy coming out of the game is black, don't try to do any cute crap. Just stick your hand out. A black sub can go through any type of scripted gyrations with another black guy coming out of the game. That's just the way it is. Don't try to be a revolutionary; you are sitting on the bench for a small college team in the middle of nowhere.

When you are not a star player on a team, it's easy to think the coach doesn't like you much. I mean, he is selecting someone else to carry out the things he or she wants done. The lineup is a perfect example of direct feedback, so when you aren't in there, it can be a little depressing and send you searching for answers to comfort your psyche. "Coach just doesn't like me" can be comforting in some cases.

Coach B never mistreated me, or any of the other non-stars, to my knowledge, but it could be tedious hearing the same things over and over when, for the most part, everything he said carried a message with it that said, "This is what you are NOT doing. This is what you are NOT capable of doing. This is why you are on the bench, and Player X is out there playing every game."

The repetition really becomes apparent by the time you are a senior, and you've heard the same teaching methods or stories for four years.

"When our guy comes off that pick, you've got to get him the ball right NOW! There's no time for a discussion or a vote. Don't ask yourself, 'Would now be a good time for me to make that pass?' It's too late if you have to think about it."

Then, he would always break into one of his favorites.

"It's like in the movies," Coach B would flip his whistle lanyard over his shoulder when he was going into one of his scripted, serious talks. He'd hold a basketball with two hands, belly high. He would make sure there were no other distractions in the gym and then take over the floor and start speaking like a lawyer making his closing argument, our team in a semi-circle like a jury in a murder trial, listening intently to every word.

"In the movies, the bad guy always has the hero pinned down. He's holding his gun, and then he decides to make a speech. Our villain then takes his sweet time telling the hero how much he's going to enjoy blowing this guy away and confesses to every crime he ever committed while you're sitting there munching your popcorn and wondering how in the world our hero is going to get out of this one. The bad guy keeps talking, and just then, the hero grabs an ax, or the screech of a far-off owl distracts the evil dude just long enough for our hero to overpower the bad guy, get the hot girl, and save Smallville from the Russians! So," Coach B would then look at us in turn and zip a fast two-handed chest pass at an unsuspecting freshman, "you've got to make that pass right now, or you're just the bad guy in another bad movie that's going to get chopped up by an ax."

"Did you notice he changed 'ax' to 'ice pick' last year?" I asked a teammate during my senior year. We got a good laugh out of that one. We made up and told several versions of Coach B's bad-guy-in-a-movie story throughout the years over dormitory card games and bus rides, but I have to admit every guy on the team knew that when a teammate was curling around a screen, he was only going to be open for a brief moment, and if you didn't make the pass immediately, a substitute would soon be at the scorer's table, and your fanny would soon be on the bench.

Just before summer's end, I was very excited to get news from the insurance agency that I had interned with that they were offering me a position. I would start right after Labor Day.

"Greetings, Joel, it's Skinny down at the agency. I've got an offer that I think you'd be interested in hearing, Joel."

Skinny always instructed me to use their first name more than once when greeting a customer or potential customer. He made it a habit, almost a trademark of his. He would pretty much always start a sentence with your first name: "Joel, can you believe this weather? Joel, I hope you had a good weekend. Joel, how are your folks getting along down in Kingman?"

The pay was going to be a slight upgrade, which welcome, as my roommates seemed to be leaving one at a time, and my expenses were climbing. I was also happy to be landing a "career" over the current "job" that I viewed the shoe store gig to be. If you run into a friend from college or while visiting your parents in your hometown, it just feels more fulfilling to say, "I'm an insurance agent at the Sanders Agency." I had also heard that Nadine got a job teaching science at some middle school in

Nebraska. They were getting a good teacher for sure. She was so smart and capable: she always had that in-charge attitude. A whole lot of me was hoping she would want to come back to Kansas before long and . . . well, be near me. Maybe she'd see my career as a pull factor. I missed her and knew I had certainly messed up a good thing. The chances of me getting a girl like Nee Nee again seemed incredibly slim, especially while I was working at a shoe store. Oh, and Titleist, yeah, I asked around and found out she was married. Shit, man. Maybe if the insurance thing got going well . . . and I kept working out . . . and I played my cards right . . . maybe then I would find a girl who would want to be my partner in this crazy thing called life.

CHAPTER EIGHT
A REAL PUBLIC SERVANT

The way Robert Clemons stood behind the bar at the House of Suds in Hutchinson, Kansas, you could tell with just one look he was not an employee. He owned the joint. His posture, his presence, his whole being projected a calm and welcoming confidence. Maybe it was the comfortable stools at the bar or the lighting in the place, the cold beer, or the décor, but most likely, it was Robert himself that, for some reason, patrons of the House of Suds tended to tell Robert what was on their hearts and minds.

"The government's got me by the balls, I'm tellin' ya."

Robert just calmly wiped the counter and moved in toward Joe Miller to let him know he was listening.

"I spent all this time getting up a bid for a remodel job over in those low-income duplexes out in that Cottonwood division," Miller said.

"Oh, yeah, over by Carey Park?" Robert asked.

"Yeah, those duplexes there," Miller continued. "Anyway, I give 'em my bid, and if I woulda known the government was even going to be involved in any way, shape, or form, I never woulda touched it. So, the super over there, a guy I've known for a while, good guy, he tells me I can get started on some demo and some layout, so I have a few days into it, and now some government guy wants to go over the whole thing with me. Puts a stop order on me. Says they have to sign off due to some of the financing being some low-interest government BS loan. I just know that little creep is going to start poking around and pulling out a flashlight and getting into crawl spaces."

A few more regulars started drifting into the tavern, and as Robert got the big screens on a few different ball games, he slid a tall glass of ice water Joe's way.

"Here, chase that beer down with this, and go see your doctor tomorrow like your daughter has been after ya to do. That will take one stress point off your plate. Then, just stay out of the government guy's way. If he makes too many demands, you adjust your bid and blame it on the government," Robert said.

"You make it sound pretty simple, Robert," Joe stated.

"That's why I'm here, Joe. To serve mankind," Robert said.

They both chuckled a little, and Robert truly hoped Joe would take his advice about the doctor. His coloring was a shade off, sort of chalky, it seemed.

CHAPTER NINE
NEE NEE'S COMEBACK

Anyone in America who remembers the mid '80s through '90s could tell you the names of the stores in their malls because, from one coast to the other, those franchise stores appeared inside these huge brick-and-mortar cathedrals to American capitalism. You could shop at Musicland or Sam Goody for your records or tapes. You could get books and gifts at Borders or Waldenbooks. Anchor stores like Sears, Dillard's, JCPenney, and Macy's provided shoppers with tons of choices. Clothing outlets like Polo, Old Navy, The Brass Buckle, and Maurices had the latest fashions. There were at least three jewelry stores, a toy store, a food court, and a movie theater in every mall. They were a small-scale Disneyland.

In the '80s and '90s, the mall was basically the town water cooler. People congregated there, and like a busy office break-room or a small-town coffee shop, people chatted, held meetings, and gossiped there. Most of the talk you would hear in these places really served no purpose, but occasionally, you could learn something valuable by hanging on the periphery of these types of rally points. In one hometown, it might have been a downtown café or post office lobby. In your hometown today, it might be a stylish coffee shop or a hip bodega. But back then, if your town had a mall, the mall took over.

So it was in the summer of '87, after I graduated, that a typical mall talk/gossip session centered on a topic I very much cared about. I was taking a short break from selling shoes or stocking shelves or what have you, and Coach B, my basketball coach for the last four years at Wesleyan, bumped into me in the food court. After a few hellos and him wanting to tell me about his new recruits that were coming to KW, he brought up Nee Nee.

"Hey, your girlfriend was sure steamed at all of us in the athletic office wasn't she!" he said, gesturing at me with a Styrofoam cup holding an Orange Julius.

I didn't say, "She's not my girlfriend anymore." But I was very interested in what he meant, so I tried to look interested but not desperate.

"You know," he continued, "she qualified for nationals, but there was no way the school was going to pay for her to go all the way to Phoenix to play a couple of girls' tennis matches. We'd have to pay for a coach and maybe a female chaperone, and there was just no way. Did she tell ya? She let us have it in the athletic office the day after graduation. Whew! That girl can make a strong argument! Howard, if you get hitched up with her, you got no chance in an argument—not that any of us guys do." He took a big slurp on the Orange Julius.

After a laugh, which I half-heartedly echoed, he closed with, "But, that doesn't make money appear. I mean, did she really think we were going to pay for her to go play in Arizona?"

I was trying not to act like I knew nothing about this, and my mind kept going back to the day she won the regional meet to qualify for nationals. She destroyed that chick from Holland. The score was 6–2, 6–1, which is like a thirty-point blowout in basketball. I watched the entire match from two courts away, trying to be inconspicuous, but I know Nee Nee knew I was there. Her strategy was brilliant. That Euro chick was so high-strung and aggressive, and Nee Nee played it so cool. Everything she did between points was like it was in slow motion. Going over to pick up a ball, she walked slowly, bent down slowly, and examined the ball slowly. In the meantime, Euro Chick was turning into Euro Spaz. The last time they played, it was just a common match. This match had something on the line. The winner advanced to nationals. You could see the added pressure mounting on Nee Nee's opponent.

At first, she was just muttering under her breath. Then she started to complain to Nee Nee with more and more vocal urgency. She would turn her palms up in the air and say, "Let's get on with it!"

She began grumbling in her native language, and by the sound of her tone, she chose her native language in order to disguise the obscene word choice.

The more she complained, the slower Nee Nee reacted. Nee Nee was bouncing the ball eight or nine times before serving instead of the conventional two to three bounces. Changeovers were lasting a full minute or more when usually it's just fifteen or twenty seconds. Nee Nee would change rackets. Tie and re-tie her shoes and mess with her socks. She'd get a different visor out of her bag, anything to slow the pace. Between points, Nee Nee was shadowing strokes like she was perfecting a mistake she had just made, and each second of delay must have felt like minutes to the intense and jumpy Dutch girl. More importantly, with each passing game, Miss Intensity was turning into Miss Inaccurate. Her shots were hitting the net or sailing out of bounds. The Dutch chick was struggling to get first serves in, and the double faults were piling up. Nee Nee was building up a huge lead.

Euro chick was ready to go Euro nuclear! In an act of pure

desperation, she called for a referee when she fell behind in the second set. A coach from a different team served as ref and calmly told the Bethany player, "She isn't violating the rules." The slower Nee Nee reacted to everything, the worse her opponent played. You didn't have to be a tennis expert to see that one player was having a mental meltdown and no matter how good her physical skills were, she had no chance of winning.

A point away from match point, Nee Nee was walking to retrieve a ball with her back to her opponent. I had a good view, and she was glowing. Glowing with accomplishment. Glowing with relief. Glowing with a goal mastered, a task complete. Her face was broadcasting a beam of happiness, and just like that, as she turned so her opponent could see her, the glow went blank. All business. Lean over deliberately and pick up the tennis ball, examine it as if the green fuzzy sphere might have something to say, all the while showing absolutely zero emotion.

I hung around for about five minutes after the match, sauntering near the edge of the court. Nee Nee was clutching a plaque and looked my way. She gave me a little mock grin with a twist of her chin, and it hit me in the gut pretty hard. Then, I could tell right away that she knew that was too mean, and she gave me the faintest of head nods to say, "I see you. You were officially here."

"She's not actually my girlfriend anymore, Coach," I managed to say. I was willing for this conversation to end.

"Oh, hmm, I didn't know that. Oh well, I guess she's already up in Hastings by now."

"Hastings? Nebraska?" I asked.

"Yeah, their middle school called and asked for references. I was in the office, and they talked to the AD and a few other people. We all gave her good references. They told us they were going to make her an offer. We didn't mention anything about her coming in and blasting us about the nationals," Coach said with a chuckle.

Yeah, because you didn't want to look bad to people from Hastings, Nebraska. Or anywhere, probably. Everybody knows that if it would have been your basketball team who qualified for nationals, you dang sure would have found a way to scrape up the money. Shit man. I wanted to talk to Nee Nee.

CHAPTER TEN
HELLO, OPERATOR?

RadioShack, located between a bookstore and a teen jeans outlet, had two kinds of telephone message machines. The expensive one had this little bitty cassette tape in it. This machine could record several minutes of telephone messages. Sixty bucks was a lot to pay when I was making $5.50 an hour, but I didn't want to miss an important phone call. Well, I didn't want to miss a call from Nee Nee. The message machine would blink a little red light if anyone left you a message, and you simply pushed a button to listen to your messages. You could save or delete the message after listening to it. It was a marvel of technology, and in the late '80s, they must have sold millions of them.

The whole telephone industry was much different than it would be just fifteen years later when digital technology overtook landlines and payphones with devices that could make phone calls from anywhere, send instant text messages, and take photos. Back then, if you didn't know someone's number, you could call a phone operator. You'd tell them what city you wanted and the name of the party you were looking for.

This conversation might go like this:

"Yes, Operator, can you give me the number for Bill Smith in York, Nebraska?"

She'd come back with, "I have a William Smith on Poplar Street and a W. J. Smith on Pine Street. Which number would you like, sir?"

"Oh, give me the one on Pine, please. What is that address?"

"That's 317 Pine Street, sir. The number is 308 blah blah blah."

"Thanks, Operator."

"For an extra twenty-five cents, I can ring the number for you."

"Oh, that won't be necessary, ma'am. Have a nice day."

"You as well, sir."

Seems easy, right? For me, it was a challenge. After running into Coach at the mall, I called the Nebraska phone operator for information.

"Hello, Operator. Can you give me a number for Nadine Blass in Hastings please?"

"That number is unlisted."

Click.

That's right. A dead end. I mean, telephone operators would tell you where people lived, their pets' names, and what night of the week they got their hair done, but if the customer filed as an unlisted number, you got nothing out of the operator. Zilch. Zero. *Click.*

Ah, but let's take a step back. I *did* gain information. I found out that Nadine did live in Hastings. And, she had a phone. So, the sixty bucks at RadioShack made perfect sense to me. She knew my phone number. We all knew at least eight or ten friends' phone numbers and probably two or three of the businesses we called most. She definitely still knew my number. Maybe she'd give me a call.

After waiting an entire half an hour after I had my answering machine hooked up, I decided to send her a card. I didn't have her address, but I could send it to the middle school where she worked. I knew the drill: call the operator, get the address of the school, and, boom, get a card in the mail to Nadine.

The mail was extremely efficient in those days, and surprisingly, Nee Nee answered my first card within a few days. I was thrilled. She said she was super busy getting ready for school, and if she got time, maybe she'd give me a call. She asked about my job. She said maybe we could even plan something on a weekend. Said to tell my folks and big sis she said hi. And she signed it, Nee Nee. Wow! She didn't give me her phone number, but maybe she would with the next card.

Any time I arrived back at my house, I would sprint to the mailbox to check for a letter or card from Nee Nee. Then, I would make a mad dash to the message machine: no blinking light.

A few weeks and two or three cards later, she wrote, *Super, super busy with school. I love my job. Hope you are well.* Still, no phone number.

Still no blinking light.

The final card arrived in mid-October: *I don't think this is a productive use of my time. Goodbye, Joel. Nadine*

CHAPTER ELEVEN
FARM BOY GOES TO TOWN

Jason and Jacob Jordan were farm boys. Their dad was a farmer, his dad was a farmer, and probably his dad too. Jason and Jacob were identical twins. They were the kind that looked alike to their teachers, I guess, but us kids could easily tell them apart. Oops, sorry about that, Mrs. Isaacs. Mrs. Isaacs was one of our English teachers, and she would say, "One of my biggest pet peeves is when people say, 'Us guys' or 'Us girls are going to do such and such.' It's 'We guys' or 'We girls.' Quit mixing up your subjects and your object pronouns! You are supposed to be farm kids, for pity's sake. You don't put your sheep in with the cattle."

Thinking about the twins really got me thinking about all kinds of school stuff. As I was saying, they were identical but not exact. They could mess with the teachers, and they did, but they couldn't fool their friends. They dressed alike until the ninth grade, no matter how much sass all the guys in our class gave them about it. Then, all it took was a comment from one girl. "Weird," she said while making a face like she was sucking on an expired pickle, and they never dressed alike again.

When the twins graduated from high school, they were given

a good-sized plot of land and the use of hundreds of thousands of dollars' worth of farm equipment. I went to college, and they went to work on their farms. We were buddies and teammates in high school, so I kept in touch with them a little bit. We'd bump into each other anytime I'd come home for a weekend or holiday break from school.

Jason was the happiest kid in the entire state of Kansas. He would always talk about how much he was enjoying getting to farm full time and not having to worry about school or some coach yelling at him for setting an illegal screen. He loved farming: the land, the risks, and the rewards. He simply loved everything that came with it.

Jacob, on the other hand, complained about every facet of farm life. He bitched about the price of fuel and fertilizer being too high and the price of wheat and soybeans being too low. Taxes? Holy cow, he criticized the government in nearly every sentence he muttered, and he cursed the weather as if cursing would change it.

I did get a scholarship that was worth $8,000. I always felt lucky that I got that.

They were given probably around a two-million-dollar business. One of them felt lucky. The other felt cursed.

Their whole farm story would sometimes hit me a little bit hard. When I was young, we lived on a farm. I can remember. I was a happy little second grader. The school bus would drop me off at our driveway, and I would skip-walk-run to our pond and skip rocks or look for frogs. Then, I would wander a different way every day, the fifty yards or so, to the east porch of our old white farmhouse. Mom would be there doing chores, always leaving at least one for me to help out with. We had two dogs and more barn cats than I could name. One of our dogs, Golden, had a special connection with me. He could tell what I was thinking, it seemed. I couldn't wait to get my own place someday and get a dog like Golden. We also had a couple of goats. Living all spread out in the country is just a way of life where you feel like you are part of the land. You're connected to nature until the school bus shows up in the morning, then you are back to real life.

Dad worked all the time. If it was light out, Dad was trying to coax as much production out of four hundred sixty acres as he possibly could while on a tractor or in a truck. If it was dark, he was in the barn or the garage working on a piece of equipment. Even at my age, I could tell he loved both time on a tractor and the challenge of fixing a broken belt on the grain truck.

I enjoyed riding along with him sometimes in the cab of our old tractor, even though the pollen made me cough and sneeze. He would talk about the crops and the land.

"Looky there, Joel," he'd brag a little. "I got those rows running darn near perfectly east and west. Gotta try to prevent those hot south winds that'll be on us soon from drying everything to dust."

I can't think of too many conversations we had back then that weren't centered on farm life.

"I gotta try to get another year out of that Massey," he'd say about our old tractor. "Didn't even get fifteen hundredths out of that shower last night, and Thompson down the road got thirty hundredths," was typical farmer talk after any kind of moisture fell on the place.

He loved dealing with seed salesmen and going to the parts store or the farm supply outlet. He did not, however, like dealing with the bank or the bankers, and that probably led to his future failings.

Those four hundred sixty acres were what was considered a small Kansas farm. In some areas of the country, maybe four hundred sixty acres was plenty to make a living from in 1979, with crops like tobacco or corn. But dryland wheat, milo, and soybeans were not going to make anyone rich on only four hundred sixty acres. If you didn't grow up on a farm, an acre is about seventy percent the size of a football field. It takes six hundred forty acres to make one square mile.

Apparently, Dad borrowed a lot of money to keep the farm going. This was borrowed money he didn't tell Mom about. Wow, was she ever mad when she found out about the loans! Interest rates were high—11, 13, even 17 percent—and two or three years of loans on crops that didn't hit the jackpot and equipment that kept breaking down spelled doom for our farm. My parents had to sell the farm to keep it from bankruptcy—the absolute worst curse word of them all to a farm family in the middle of America.

Jacob and Jason's dad, Mr. Jordan, bought our farm. The day after they bought it, they burned down the house and the barn. Acreage is what they were after. The shabby pole shed we called the garage became a place to store some equipment. They planted their new ground within weeks. They were good operators, and their equipment wouldn't be breaking down. They wouldn't be borrowing money at outrageous interest rates. They wouldn't be packing up all their stuff in a borrowed truck and moving into a crowded neighborhood.

We moved about ten miles into town and rented a little house in Kingman, Kansas. We had a next-door neighbor named Daniel. Shirtless Dan is what Dad called him. Every time he looked at me, I was scared. He was a mean person, and he wanted me to know he was a mean person. One time, I was just dribbling a basketball on our sidewalk. He leaned his head out his front door and said, "Knock off the racket, you little shit." From then on, I would walk a couple of blocks to the park anytime I wanted to play outside. The landlord wouldn't let us have a dog, and there was no barn for barn cats. The Jordans even bought our goats. Dad said we needed every dime we could get to stay out of bankruptcy.

Dad got a couple of different jobs in town over the years. So did Mom. I never saw them happy again like they were on the farm.

CHAPTER TWELVE
FROM SKIP TO SKINNY

The finality of that last note from Nee Nee sent me into a spiral of doomsday thoughts. My days were spent either working at the mall or working at the insurance agency. I took the licensing exam and passed it on the first attempt, so that was probably the only green light I had in my life. I felt like I was floundering. On nights I didn't work at the mall, I wound up drinking too much at Coach's, a sports bar a few blocks down the street from the mall. Coach's Bar and Grill was close enough to my house and work that I could walk if I wanted. That was probably part of the problem. "Sure, I'll have a few more beers. I can just walk home from here," I'd think out loud as I sat at the bar near closing time.

My manager at the insurance agency went by the name of Skinny. I never heard him go by anything else. I noticed on his state insurance license hanging in his office that his real name was Leonard or Leon or something like that, but anyway, Skinny was always talking to me about when he was going to bump me up to full-time, but he never would mention specific dates. He was paying me six bucks an hour, and it wasn't amounting to much in the bank account. When I was in the office, I spent my time going through old files and calling clients.

"Just check in on 'em. See those notes? If it says they got two boys and he likes Chevy trucks, you just chat him up about how those boys' flag football team is doing and if he's still hanging on to that Chevy," Skinny would explain.

Sometimes, I would go out on a sales call with him to try for new business or service an account that needed renewal or additions. I felt like I was doing a good job as an assistant and was learning the ropes quite well for an apprentice. I wanted to press him for a definitive date and details like salary and job duties, but I didn't want to press too hard and seem pushy.

Finally, in early November, Skinny sidled up to me while I was on the phone with a potential client. He motioned with his hand and over-exaggerated with his lips, "In my office." I can read lips fairly well, but not when people exaggerate. When I was a kid, we would watch movies at home with the sound turned all the way down to try to get as proficient as Marilyn at reading lips. She was way better than Mom and me. Dad never really tried.

I went into Skinny's office as quickly as I could, and a pretty big wave of nerves hit me when he told me to shut the door.

Skinny had some small, framed family photos and one of those golf tee puzzles shaped like a triangle on his desk. "You know, Joel, it seems you've been hanging out at Coach's a lot lately."

My focus quickly went from that little golf tee puzzle to exactly what Skinny was saying. Oh, shit, man, he was going to give me a lecture. I was hoping for a salary, and he was going to give me a friggin' lecture. Dang. I felt like a bench player again.

"Now, Joel, it's okay for a businessman to be social. I encourage it. But," he leaned in and steepled his fingers toward me, "you want to be known as a businessman. An *insurance* man, Joel. A man a family can trust to help them with hefty decisions in their lives. Mortgages, Joel. Finances. Joel, those are big-ticket items to any family man. You don't want to be known as just some guy who drinks a lot, and oh, by the way, he also works down there at the Sanders Agency."

I nodded, and it was a little hard to admit, but Skinny was right. I sort of felt like Coach B had just told me I had to do a better job of defending against the baseline dribble drive. It was true; I was spending too much time sitting on a bar stool every night. I was about to say something to validate Skinny and try to lift myself up as well. The words were a little slow coming to my lips. No need to stare at the floor. I needed to look Skinny in the eye and tell him I'd be a better man going forward.

"Things are in order now, Joel, for you to go full-time on December 1," Skinny said.

I couldn't believe my ears! This was great news. A salary. An office. We had a secretary and everything. Skinny had said he would be retiring in three to five years, and if I was capable, that big office and his nice, big book of business and the lion's share of the commissions that go along with it might all be mine. I'm telling ya, a mind can go through lots of stuff at a crazy high rate of speed. I had just heard that Allen Wagner, the top scorer on our basketball team, was having real trouble finding a job. Ha! I had to sit there on the bench and watch him score all those points, and now he could just sit and watch me climb in the business world!

After a few minutes of Skinny reminiscing about his early days in the insurance business, Skinny explained how the changes would work. I wouldn't be getting a salary. I would be getting a "draw." It's like a salary, except that future commissions I earned would get paid back. Skinny said it would take about six months, probably, to get me on my feet and get some commissions rolling in.

"You give it a few months, then you'll get rolling. You'll get what we call *traction* in this business. Once you get some traction, you can really get things going your way. You'll be a crackerjack agent, Joel."

He would get an appointment with a professional photographer lined up for me, pronto. My "professional headshot," he kept calling it. Business cards, placards, flyers, ads in the *Salina Journal*, ads on AM and FM radio stations; he was getting me kind of excited talking about the promotional side of things. All in all, it was a great afternoon. I would need to tell Manager David that my last day at the shoe store would be sometime before December 1. *Whew.* I needed some good news for sure.

I left Skinny's office with a grin the size of Texas, and Skinny's secretary, Lynne, had a nice smile too.

I found David in the back room, breaking down some cardboard boxes. He was truly happy for me. "I could tell you didn't want to stay in retail forever, Joel. The timing of this is pretty crazy because I just got a call about you today from Skip."

Skip was our regional manager (yep, the "oh, shit" guy). He oversaw about ten stores in Kansas and Oklahoma.

"Skip was asking if I thought you'd be able to train a newbie in the Hutchinson store. It's only an hour away, and they are experiencing some turnover and just need some management help. The timing might be a little tight because it would mean you working Black Friday in Hutchinson and staying there for about a week to get their new staff ready to run on their own."

I was taking this in and just trying to make the calendar work in my head. I would be going to Mom's for Thanksgiving, and it was only forty-five minutes from the Hutchinson Mall. David's calendar was right in sync with mine.

"Corporate will put you up in a nice place. I think they have a brand-new Hampton Inn in Hutchinson. You'll get twenty-five bucks a day for food and miscellaneous. Cash. You'll work all day Black Friday, and then Skip will be there to help out on Saturday." David leaned back on the counter in the back room. "You'll need to put in a lot of hours over that Thanksgiving weekend, but the pay will be good. We need to do whatever it takes to get their people on board. The new hires are pretty sharp, so by Thursday or Friday the next week, you could be done. Skip and I will keep a close eye on 'em after that until they have it down."

That would still give me a few days off to enjoy before my December 1 start date with the Sanders Agency as a *businessman*. Twenty-five bucks a day to eat on? I could easily eat for seven or eight bucks a day and pocket the rest! This was going to be awesome.

We would work out the arrangements in the next day or two David said. "I gotta get busy," David said. "Need to let Skip know we got this, and I have to schedule some interviews and find someone to replace you. Sheesh, I'm going to be busier than the liquor store on New Year's Eve. I've got Black Friday without you. Oh well, at least I won't have to worry about Skip popping in the back door since he'll be with you!"

We both grinned, and at the same time, said, "Oh, shit!" and shared a good belly laugh.

After we closed that night, I walked the bag down to the drop slot, made a little small talk with the assistant manager from the toy store, and decided to drive straight home. Nine in the morning would come quickly, and I needed to get some rest, but by the time I was parking alongside my house, an old house divided into three apartments, I decided I had time to walk over to Coach's Sports Bar and celebrate a little bit.

Look at my good fortunes: a new position at the agency, getting put up in a hotel with first-class treatment, and getting to train some rookies. Maybe I'd meet the right girl while I was in Hutchinson.

Sure would be nice to find a bar like Coach's in Hutchinson. It had four big screens with four different games on, but the best part was that there was no sound booming from any of the screens. Anybody who goes to a sports bar to watch a game doesn't need to be told, "The nose of the ball is resting just past the fifty-yard line." Sports fans can see that the dang ball is at the fifty! That way, you can talk and, better yet, listen to your buddies. I hate a bar where you have to yell or have someone yell at you just to hear, "How ya doin', Joel?"

I was wearing only a light jacket, but I didn't need to run back into the house to get a proper winter coat. November nights can be cold in Kansas, but usually, it's mild until the middle of December. That's when winter decides to stop and stay a while. I decided to walk through a different neighborhood this time and was pleased to find it was a little better than my usual trek to my favorite hangout. There were almost no street-lights, but the sidewalks were much smoother than my other route, so maybe I'd avoid jamming my toe into the raised edge of some six-inch crack in settling cement.

Petey was working the bar. When your last name is Peterson and you work at a sports bar, you are going to be called Pete or Petey; it's just the way it is. But I'm the kind of guy who likes to come up with his own nicknames, so a while back, I had started calling Petey "Alfalfa."

Petey had given me a strange look, but only for a second. Then he lifted his chin and grinned. I thought he was going to say, "Ah. Okay, from *Our Gang*," making my reference ring true. Petey was the dog on the old children's show, and Alfalfa was one of the other characters.

But all he said was, "Well, okay, Opie."

My brain was spinning for a while. Opie was a character on *The Andy Griffith Show*. Ron Howard played Opie. Aha. Joel Howard became Opie at Coach's that day. It wasn't the worst nickname a guy could have. When Petey—er, Alfalfa—stuck a nickname on a guy in his bar, there was no wiggling off that hook. If he said your name was Mud, well, you better like everyone there calling you Mud.

I walked in and two or three guys looked up. "Hey Opie, how's it going? Have you watched the Coyotes play yet this year? Coach B got any size on that team?" We chatted for about a minute or two, and then Alfalfa asked me, "Tall or pint tonight, Opie?"

"I'll just have a Pepsi," I said, feeling Skinny's drift from his lecture that morning.

About an hour passed by, and it was getting on past eleven, and who walks in the door? Skinny Sanders. He was with his wife, and when he saw me, he had sort of a surprised, "What in the world?" look on his face. His wife was all smiles.

"Oh, hi, Joel. We're celebrating a little tonight. There's not many places to go this late," she said while her husband Skinny looked totally awkward and out of place.

I wanted to make sure Skinny saw that I was following his instructions and just being social. "Hey, Skinny. I'm having Pepsi, but I'd be happy to get you and the missus a drink or an appetizer if you'd like to join me."

She was about to accept with a nod and a grin when Skinny interrupted and said, "No, thanks, Joel, really, but we are just going to have us some quiet time over there at a booth in the corner. Good to see you, young man."

Young man? Sounded weird coming from Skinny the way it did. He was always so calm and in charge. Of course, all our conversations occurred in his office or his Volvo wagon while out on appointments. Always his space. In the office, he'd lift a framed photo of a family member and tell some little anecdote connected to that person, or he'd point to a story in the *Salina Journal*. "Did you read this story yet, Joel? You gotta read about this."

Maybe Skinny felt out of his element in the bar scene. Maybe he felt like he was on my stomping grounds, and it made him uncomfortable. Or maybe he was pissed when the first person he saw at the bar was the one person he definitely told to stay *out* of bars. I was his employee, and I was just flaunting my non-compliance in his face. Man, the more I sat there with my Pepsi, the more worried I got.

I decided to at least stop by his booth on the way out. You know, make eye contact and say a few things to let him know he wasn't handing the keys to the business he'd built over the past twenty-seven years to a blitzed-out-of-his-mind drunk.

"Alfalfa," I called out. "Can you get me a basket of popcorn?"

"Sure thing, Opie."

I took a final swig of my Pepsi—oh, the draft beers the regulars were drinking did look good—and grabbed the basket of fresh popcorn. I walked over to the corner booth and slid the basket between Skinny and his wife.

"You two have a wonderful evening," I said. "See ya tomorrow afternoon, Skinny."

I simply cannot remember her name, but Skinny's wife was very grateful. "Oh, you're too kind, Joel. No wonder Skinny speaks so highly of you."

Skinny looked so uncomfortable as he squirmed in his seat, fidgeting and fighting any semblance of eye contact while sending me some pretty strong "not now, Joel!" vibes.

As I walked home, I was consumed with thoughts about the weird encounter with Skinny. First off, I was super glad that I hadn't pounded down four or five beers before he got there. I hadn't known him for long, but he was so uncomfortable, and yet his wife was so happy. It was topsy-turvy. Was he about to dump some bad news on her? Was he going to divorce her on the spot? I hoped they liked the popcorn. I had never seen Skinny not be the man of the room, comfortable and confident. He always exuded expert, well-dressed businessman charm. What a weird experience to see him unsure of himself.

I was keeping my head down, following the dark sidewalk home, when I heard a door open and a voice say, "Get out there and do your business, Ringo."

The door was pulled closed, and a little four-legged pet pranced out into his dimly lit backyard and headed near the chain link fence I was walking past to "do his business."

"Holy cow," I said right out loud. A mini rat terrier, just like the guy from Kansas City with the critter extraction business. "Hi, Ringo. Hi, buddy," I said in that stupid, typical, "he's such a good boy" voice we humans somehow think is Dog—sort of like how people in America put an "el" in front of a word and they think they are speaking Spanish.

Ringo gave me a little look, the way dogs tilt their head, and then focused on what he was there to do. He gave me another friendly look with welcoming eyes, and I thought of my dog Golden. A dog's eyes can make a guy just melt if they have that accepting glow. Ah, what a nice way to end my evening.

"See ya, Ringo," I said. This time, I didn't use that goofy talk. I guess I didn't want Ringo to think I was an idiot.

I looked in front of the house to see if the guy had a truck with a business sign on it touting critter extraction. No such sign. No such truck.

The next day the shit hit the fan. A lot of shit. And multiple fans.

CHAPTER THIRTEEN
SHIT HAPPENS

My "day of shit," as I have ever since referred to it, started off pretty normal and on a positive note. I went in to open the shoe store. All the normal things were happening in a normal manner. I opened the back door. The key worked. The light switch fired up the humming sounds of the fluorescent lighting. I did a quick check of our shelves and displays, tossed some trash in a container, and was opening up the back door when I heard the UPS truck on the back dock. Sure enough, we received several large boxes of stock. My back-room gal would be there by noon to take care of that. Got the cash drawer all set up, and the clock told me I had fifteen minutes before open. Just time enough to call home and tell Mom all my news and remind her that I wanted raisins in the stuffing again this year and to get it a little crispy on the edges. Oh, how I love my mother's Thanksgiving stuffing and her mashed potatoes.

I picked up the office phone on the small desk we used to manage the shoe store. "Collect, from Joel," I told the operator.

In a few seconds and after a click or two, I was hoping to hear my mom's voice accept the charges, but it was Dad.

"Yeah, sure, I'll just keep paying for him," he said gruffly.

"Hey, Dad, how's it going?" I asked, trying not to be bothered by the dig.

"Oh, it's fine. How's the shoe business? You guys making any big moves on the New York Stock Exchange?" he asked sarcastically.

I don't know what he expected out of me. I never did know.

"I actually called to tell Mom I'd be home for Thanksgiving. Just tell her to call me tonight. Any time after six, I should be home. G'bye, Dad," I said, trying to end the call before he could land another zinger.

"Woah, wait a minute," Dad's voice turned intense. "I'm the one paying for this call. So, are you planning on staying up there in Salina? Even now, with school being over for you?"

"Well," I stammered a little. I wanted to tell Mom about the agency job. They knew I was part-time after passing the test, but I wanted to tell them how I was going to be a real, bona fide, full-time insurance agent. He would question and doubt. Mom would accept and believe. "Yeah, for now. I'm doing okay. I have some friends and—"

"You have friends here too, Joel. Come back down here to Kingman or Hutchinson, or hell, even Wichita. Why ya wanna stay . . ." he continued to drone on, and I tuned him out.

I could tell this wasn't really going anywhere. I really wanted to tell Mom, but I let Dad get the best of me, so I blurted out, "I'm going full-time for the insurance agency. My last day at the shoe store is next week."

Silence on Dad's end.

"I better get going, Dad."

"You're just a fucking big shot up there, eh?" he snapped.

I had *never* heard my dad use that language. Maybe a damn or a hell. Maybe a bullshit if we were watching the Chiefs play the Raiders.

"What did you play? A total of maybe five games if you strung 'em all together and you think you're some kind of fucking local celeb that people will flock to and buy their insurance? You can send 'em a little Christmas card with your picture on it the way all these fucking insurance vultures and bankers do. I guess they think we wanna see their face every time we turn around. Hang a banner at some horseshit bowling alley with your cute little grin on it. That will prove you know insurance! Get yourself a nice three-hundred-dollar suit and ring a fucking Salvation Army bell for thirty minutes in front of the grocery store on a busy day. Hey, everyone! Look at me, Mr. *Businessman,*" he spat. "I'll tell your mother you called."

Good Lord, he'd never unloaded that kind of venom on me . . . or anyone, as far as I knew. Why was he so angry at me? Was he angry at Mom too? Did he treat her like that all the time? I'd been gone four years . . . and when I was home, I was in high school. When you're in high school, you don't pay attention to anything. I flashed back to Nee Nee's mom and dad. Was he drinking? Did my dad have a drinking problem I didn't know about? Did we have alcoholism in our family? Beer did seem to get a hold on me sometimes.

"Come on, we've got time for a quick cup." Joy, our super-employee, was ready to clock in and help get the store running for the day even though she would soon be off for maternity leave. We normally would make a coffee run at 9:50 a.m. and open the doors at 10 a.m. sharp.

"Okay, sure." I tried to appear normal as I came out of the back room in a fog from talking to—well, listening to my dad blow up. "Joy, I'll get yours. Decaf, right?" And I didn't mean to direct my eyes down to her obviously pregnant belly, but . . .

"No, I'll go with you, maybe get this baby movin' in the right direction. Due date is in eleven days. Eleven minutes would be fine with me," she said, laughing but not joking.

As a clueless guy who knew absolutely nothing about babies and birthing, I just tried to keep my eyes straight ahead and my mouth shut, silently praying that kid wasn't popping out of there in eleven minutes.

We briskly walked down the corridor while the soft Christmas music was filling the spaces. Even though Joy was totally pregnant, she still had a quick pace about everything she did. Some stores were already showing off their Christmas glitz. You could get a cup of java at four or five places, but today, we were in a hurry, so we went to the closest place, a cookie company, and got in line behind the big wig from the bank. I was wearing my typical mall manager uniform, short-sleeved shirt and tie, with dark slacks, while he was wearing a very nice —and I'm sure immensely expensive—suit. It made me think about what my dad had just said about bankers and insurance men.

Mr. Big Wig Banker seemed to be getting agitated about his coffee order. "No. Just . . . yes. I said two. Here, just give me the packet thingies, and I'll put 'em in there myself."

As I peered around him, I noticed the young man trying to fill the order. He was obviously new, and judging by his fidgety fingers and wobbly legs, he had a mega-size case of anxiety. And then, by his posture and other signals, I knew it just before he turned, and I saw his hearing aids. He was hearing impaired.

After another sigh and a grunt, Mr. Banker looked into his coffee cup, turned and gestured the cup my way, shook his head from left to right, and said, "The simplest of requests. What a fuckin' retard." He looked back into his coffee cup, made a *pfft* sound in disgust, and walked his way toward the bank, where he would sit down and make more money in one hour than this young man who had tried his best would make if he worked from open to close.

I let that suit stop me!

When he said that disgusting remark, he thought I was on his side! For some reason, he looked at me and decided I was on *Team Asshole*. Of course, he was the captain, that was obvious with his Alpha clothing and demeanor. Still, he looked at me as if we were in this together. *Let's go be jerks to anyone who doesn't instantly serve us with the respect and deference we deserve. We've earned it. Can't you see this suit?*

Shit. I was so mad at myself. I ordered a coffee, and Joy got hers too.

There were a hundred things I could have done or said, but I swear I let that suit beat me. Easily a hundred things. One, I could have taken my right fist and slammed it into his left jaw with enough force to send his coffee flying and his pretty, tailored suit skidding across the freshly cleaned quarry tile floors that were the pride of every spiffy new mall.

Two, I could have said, "Woah, jackass, where do you get off being so rude? Apologize to this young man."

Three, oh three through a hundred, why didn't I do or say something? Anything?

On the way back to the store, Joy tried to quickly tell me about a time her sister tried to get a loan from that bank to buy a Chevy Blazer. "He's just the biggest jerk in the world." She said some other things, but my mind was in a fog. I kept wondering how many times that kid had been put down like that, and then I thought of Marilyn. Had people been rude to her like that? I know that when she was fresh out of high school, finding a job was really hard for her. I wondered what kind of insults had been tossed her way.

That damn suit.

And what did I do? Nothing. Just like always.

And his shoes. He didn't get those shoes at Kinney Shoes in some mall. Those things came from downtown, maybe even Kansas City.

I was pretty steamed at myself throughout the day. I wanted to go down to the bank and just handle things. I wanted to do a million things, but I didn't. I was going to be glad when three o'clock came around, and I could clock out of my mall world and head over to my business world to see if Skinny needed any help with anything.

Oh, Skinny. Sheesh. He was so weird last night.

Skinny last night. My dad this morning. Big shot banker man. The deaf kid. Me.

Yes, shit hit the fan that morning. And the hits just kept on coming.

There I was, working along at the shoe store. At about two in the afternoon, things were pretty normal, and considering it was a Wednesday, we had a good flow of customers, which always made the day go better. So, there I was at the cash register, sliding the credit card machine over someone's Visa card, when I looked up and saw two familiar faces from the past—make that four faces.

The Jordan twins, Jason and Jacob. Jason, the happy farmer, and his brother Jacob, the complainer. Actually, they both looked pretty happy at the moment. They were doing some Christmas shopping, and they had their ladies with them.

When I saw the two happy couples, my mind went into a major flashback—a flashback about Nadine. Dang, she was smart. Dang. Nee Nee was right about everything. Why did a major Nadine flashback hit me? Because there stood Jason and Jacob with Isabella Dubois and Haley Schott. Isabella Dubois was a year behind us in school, homecoming queen, smart, cute, and married Jason twelve months after her high school graduation. Haley Schott was a little harder to figure. She was a rich girl who went to a neighboring school. She was a friend of Isabella, and that's what got her hooked up with Jacob. She went to a JUCO for a year, and then, as Jacob liked to brag, "She wanted an M-R-S degree more than a BS degree."

While the two farmers were standing there with their cute wives, I caught a glimpse of the sideways look they shared. Their grin said it all. *Well, Joel was the best athlete in school, but here* *he is, making $16,000 a year, maybe, while we drive brand new trucks and make a killing in the ag business.*

Talk about traction.

They were giving me a mocking chuckle, but all I could hear was Nadine's voice. It was a night in the dorm early in my junior year. Like almost every night, a bunch of us guys were playing cards in the lobby. The lobby would divide itself into two major groups of play. The African American guys would play dominoes —"bones," they called it. The white guys played ten-point pitch. Nadine and a few other girls would come by and visit maybe once or twice a week. They would jump in and play cards for a while and then be off. One night, while we were playing ten-point pitch, this girl who had never come to our wing of the dorm stopped in. She tried to learn how to play pitch but wasn't very successful. Her name was Anne. She left after about half an hour.

"See ya, Anne," a couple of guys said.

"She's cool," said another.

"That was nice of her to give us a visit," one guy said. "I hope she joins our games more often."

"You guys are so stupid," said Nadine. And she held the "oo" sound in "stupid" just long enough to make it sound like a curse word.

While delivering this verdict, Nadine shook her head a certain way like she just discovered we didn't know two plus two is four. I wanted to say, "Woah. I got a three-point-three here, and Scooter there is on the four-point-oh Dean's List." But I couldn't say anything because I was all caught up in how the dark color of her inner eyes made the whites of her eyes look whiter than Christmas Eve snow. I still remember, she was wearing a white blouse, starched, and it was having a contest with those eyes to see which could attract me more. Her eyes and her strength didn't back down one bit. Good Lord, she was beautiful.

Scooter shot back, "Oh, whatever, Nadine. So, we waste some time playing cards. We could be out on the street doing worse things."

"It's not that," Nadine said. "It's Anne. She's never coming back here. You guys are all like, 'She's so nice, I hope she comes back.' Sheesh. You know what this week is, don't you?"

After a pause just long enough for us guys to look at each other like, "Is it some weird holiday or religious week we've never heard of?"

"It's *homecoming week*. She's up for queen. Right now, she's on first floor west asking how to put antifreeze in her car, and in an hour, she'll be on the second floor of Wilson asking dumb questions there."

All of us guys just came to a stop and stared at each other. She was probably right. We hadn't given it a thought that we'd be voting for homecoming queen in a day or two.

"Huh," Scooter said, "subtle campaigning. I gotta give her credit."

One other guy said, "I'm voting for her either way. I'll bid seven."

I didn't say anything because all I could think of was how, when, and where I was going to ask Nadine out on a date. Dang, those eyes. They were just right, and the way they sat above her cheeks was like an artist designed an ideal logo for a company called Perfectly Gorgeous Woman. I wanted to grab the tips of the collar on her crisply starched blouse and pull them to my face.

Remembering Nee Nee, both her intellect and her beauty, was a tough shot of reality. Making it tougher was me looking at these two good-looking chicks who had played their homecoming queen card just right. They'd never look at these two guys for more than five seconds if they didn't own a zillion acres of land. Nee Nee would've done that little shake of her head. I could hear her saying, "You guys are so stupid." She said it to all of us guys.

One of the Jordan wives bought some waterproofing spray we sold to protect leather boots and handbags. They left, taking their mocking attitudes with them, but my day of shit and fans was not over.

Only a couple more weeks of lines like, "Those have a reinforced upper that will give you comfort all day." After I got off duty at the shoe store, I made a quick detour through Dillard's to check out some of the menswear. I would need a few new ties and some quality slacks and shirts for my entrance into the world of selling insurance. I had one decent blazer, but I remember taking it off after our sports banquet last spring and thinking, "This thing is at the end of its lifespan."

There were plenty of good looks available. I figured I would get a couple of white shirts and then maybe a light blue one and one dark gray or black one. Black and gray slacks go with about everything, so that would be a good choice. A blazer could wait a while. I remembered that Nee Nee had given me a couple of great-looking tops for Christmas. Then, on the way out of the department store, the fragrance of those scented potpourri bags they sell hit me. Nee Nee's apartment always smelled so good. Dang, I couldn't get her out of my mind today.

I stopped off at my house—no blinking light. Shoot. Checked the mail, but nothing. So, I changed clothes and headed down to the Sanders Agency for a little on-the-job training. I thought about getting donuts for the office or some flowers for Lynne, our secretary, but I was sort of in a hurry. Lynne was the quintessential receptionist. She could make anyone feel warm and welcome.

I knew that when I walked in the door, Lynne would say, "Hello, Joel. Good to see you again. How is your day going?"

Well, I could be truthful and say, "Well, actually, Lynne, it's been probably the shittiest day in the last several years for me. My dad gave me a bunch of crap today over the phone. Then, some asshole from the bank called a defenseless kid a vulgar name, and I was right there, and I did absolutely nothing about it. So, I'm feeling pretty shitty about myself. That all happened before 10 a.m. Then, let's see, I saw a couple of so-called friends from high school who mocked me for working in a shopping mall shoe store while they enjoyed their life of leisure with a couple of nice-looking babes. Oh, and the babes reminded me that I'm single with very little chance of that changing any time soon.

"So, how's my day, Lynne? I'd say it's about nine toilets on a scale of one to ten for crap. How has your day been so far?" I could have said that.

But Lynne didn't ask me how my day was. In fact, when I walked in, she got a startled look on her face, spun 180 degrees in her chair, and walked directly to the Xerox machine. I quietly greeted Lynne and advanced past the leather furniture in the waiting room toward Skinny's office. There was an awkward-ness hanging in the air that made me feel like I was walking across a pond with ice too thin to support my weight. The office door was open about three inches, and his head was down, working on some paperwork. I gave a quiet, two-knuckle knock on the half-open door, and Skinny waved me in.

When I left the office ten minutes later, I could tell that Lynne had been crying. She did not look up at me.

Let me give you the condensed version. Skinny's daughter—I guess he thought I needed proof that he had a daughter with four kids because he showed me her picture. Anyway, this daughter's husband had been with a Chrysler dealership for about fifteen years down in Tulsa. Apparently, he got sideways with the owners of this car dealership and was now unem-ployed. So Skinny and his daughter had decided that they would be moving to Salina and he would be working at the Sanders Agency. "Joel, I guess I won't have that position for you after all.

I wish you good luck. Lynne will send your last paycheck in the mail. You don't have to take the time to come down for it."

That's why Skinny and his wife had been celebrating last night at Coach's Bar and Grill. Their daughter and grandkids were going to be moving to Salina. Well, shit.

I guess my mind has a way of ranking things. I have my favorite hamburger at a little burger shop called Bogeys. They have several posters of Humphrey Bogart hanging on the wall, and I don't know if it's the decor or the fries or the burgers themselves, but everything just goes together so well in there, and I just love it. My least favorite would be the Big Mac from McDonald's (they won't be upset to discover this as they seem to be doing fine in the business world). My favorite holiday is the Fourth of July, and my least favorite is Christmas. So, automatically, I began ranking this day on a scale of shittiness. Was this my shittiest day ever? It was right up there. It had several elements that usually exist when days turn to shit.

1. Family angst: Definitely checks this box. Dad gave me crap this morning, which also made me feel sad for Mom. Anytime I see a deaf or hearing-impaired person, I think of Marilyn, and this always makes me feel bad for the times I ignored her. So, yep today was an overflowing truckload of family angst.

2. Money problems: Money is often at the root of personal uneasiness. It's hard to relax and face tomorrow when the constant tug of money problems distracts and gnaws at your inner being. Well, good thing I didn't buy the ties and slacks at Dillard's that morning because I wouldn't be sitting for a professional photographer and getting a headshot. *And*, I had told David I was leaving my job at the shoe store, *and* he was probably filling my spot as I was walking out the door at the Sanders Agency.

3. Relationship problems: Nadine was gone. She wasn't coming back. That light on my message machine wasn't going to be blinking when I walked in the door of my apartment. I wasn't a "productive use of her time," or however she put it. She was gone. It was final. Having no resources to speak of, I wasn't on the radar of some chick from college or my hometown or anywhere, quite frankly.

4. Thoughts of revenge: That fucking banker. The one this morning and the one from my childhood. I remember Mom being so upset when my dad borrowed all that money from the bank. She said, "Why would they loan you that kind of money? There was no way our acreage could support that. They hold all the chips now. They can break it up and sell it for more, or they can subdivide it for housing. They win no matter what."

Skinny Sanders. I guess he's not a man of his word. His daughter gives him a call, and boom, he throws me out onto the street. I guess they have connections. Like the twins and all their farmland, they are connected. They know how to network. Their connections turned Great-Grandpa's one hundred sixty acres into the sections, thousands of acres, they own today. They aren't renting out of a rundown, old triplex. They had the inside lane. The banker probably called them first when they saw Dad couldn't keep up with the payments. Just like that Anne chick who won homecoming queen, the Jordans knew who to network with to get the right calls and make the right moves. They weren't the ones losing their farmland or losing their jobs at an insurance agency or a shoe store. I bet they'd grin when they heard about that.

And that's the thought that stopped me. A week ago, I was the one grinning that Allen Wagner couldn't find a job and I was "moving up" in the world. My mind went right ahead with some valid logic and truthfulness.

Dear Joel, you really need to hear this from yourself: Allen Wagner got to play more and scored more points than you because he was stronger down low with the ball than you were. If you wanted to get stronger, there was a weight room open dang near twenty-four hours a day, and you could have been in there more. Dear Joel, Nadine decided she didn't want to be with you anymore. That is her business. You broke up with a girl a few months before seeing Nadine. You told that girl, "We just don't see eye to eye on things," and you told your friends, "She basically has shit for brains." So, maybe Nadine decided you don't see eye to eye or maybe she decided you have shit for brains, or something entirely different, but either way, she's gone and it's not her fault. You didn't lift the weights, you didn't ask Nadine how she was feeling, and you didn't provide support for your sister. Joel, it's time you started doing things to make a difference instead of observing what goes on and then complaining about the outcome.

That's the day. That shitty, shitty day. That's the day I decided to rob the bank.

CHAPTER FOURTEEN
CALL 911

"Oh my God, they're playing Christmas songs on the radio already! I'm gonna need two baskets of Robert's mushrooms and some cold beer tonight," Steven Sawyer said right out loud to himself as he drove his pickup truck through the south end of Hutchinson. "It will be turkey for days on end soon, so I better get me some catfish too."

Steven Sawyer rolled up to the House of Suds in South Hutch like he normally did a few times a week, but this time, something was off. As Sam walked up to the front door, he saw Joe Miller's work truck parked diagonally in front of the bar, but there was something about Miller's truck that was off-kilter. As he approached, he figured it out. The truck was on but not running. He could hear the radio and a buzzer, maybe the seat belt beeper, and the lights were on, but the engine was not running. And . . . Joe Miller was not sitting at the wheel.

As Sam got a little closer, he saw that Miller was, in fact, sitting at the wheel, but he was slumped over to his right, lying across the console that separated the bucket seats of the Dodge truck.

Steven was trying to come up with a funny little line. "Did you drop your Girl Scout cookies, Joe?" or some such opener, but it was cold, and anyway, he could find someone to tease inside. He peered in the truck, and then he could see enough clues to know that Joe Miller was not just looking for something he dropped between the console and the seat, and he may not even be conscious.

Steven tried the door, but it was locked. He banged on the window a couple of times before he hustled inside the tavern and announced loudly, "Hey, Joe Miller is having a health issue out here. Somebody, quick, call 911. His truck is locked, and he needs assistance."

That got heads turning at the bar and from a few booths where both the usuals and some infrequent customers were enjoying a quiet evening out of the cold. The barkeep quickly dashed back through the swinging cutout in the bar, picked up the landline telephone, and called 911. A determined gal crossed the floor from a circular high-top table, saying, "I'll call his daughter Debra. She may have a spare key."

"The ambulance won't need a key. They'll just bust their way in," an onlooker said.

"If it was your dad, I bet you'd beat the ambulance here, don't ya think?" the determined gal said, and she was in the phone booth and then off the phone in no time. "Debra's on her way," she announced quite loudly, her voice clearly broadcasting the pride of a job well done.

"We could bust the window," one customer calmly said.

"He might just be sleeping. He had more than a few," another customer said.

For the record, Joe's daughter Debra, who lived maybe six blocks from the bar, raced up and searched under the back wheel well on the driver's side and found a small magnetic box designed to hold a key. She used the key to open the truck, which set the panic horn on the truck into a honking fit. By the time the ambulance arrived, probably five minutes after Debra, Joe was laid out on the sidewalk with his friends attempting

CPR. Most of them knew they were too late. Joe's color was all gone in his face, and he simply had no life left in him.

The ambulance crew took over and attempted to restore Joe, but after about fifteen minutes, everyone there knew the verdict. Joe Miller had bid his last job and told his last good story down at the House of Suds. Joe Miller was gone from this life.

CHAPTER FIFTEEN
THE PLAN

Now, I told you at the beginning that I was the luckiest guy in North America. That's true, but robbing the bank wasn't luck. Robbing the bank was just planning and executing a plan without any bad luck intervening. Some plans are simpler than others, but I just saw it as a plan. A plan that came together in my mind over a few months and presented itself as a tangible task. The luck took place later.

Thanksgiving was in eight days. The Wednesday before Thanksgiving was my last day at the mall in Salina. David had hired someone, and I wasn't going to dump my troubles on him. He gave that person a job. That person was getting their life in order based on getting that job. I wasn't going to interfere. I was scheduled to work at the Hutchinson Mall from Black Friday through the next week until, according to the district manager, "Thursday or Friday, whenever we can tell that these guys are ready to take the training wheels off." I was going to rob the bank in Salina on Black Friday. I had some things to put in order.

MONDAY

Monday before Thanksgiving rolled around, and I had some shopping to do after clocking out of the shoe store at 3 p.m. In the '80s, perhaps the most popular winter coat was a navy blue, quilt-lined, vinyl zip-up that had a hood with a mock fur halo. It had a flap you could button across your chin for those cold Kansas nights. It sold at Walmart for just under $30. A pair of cheap winter gloves, black, went for $2.99. I purchased these at the Walmart in McPherson, Kansas, which is located about halfway between Salina and Hutchinson. Nobody in McPherson knew me. Nobody would be able to say, "Yes, I sold a coat and gloves to Joel Howard a few days before that bank got robbed."

There's a thrift shop in McPherson too. They had a used stepstool, the metal kind that folds up, with only two steps. That is exactly what I needed. It was two bucks. Sold. I picked up a heavy, used quilt for another two bucks. They had a stocking cap that you could pull down over your face with holes in it for eyes, nose, and mouth. I only worried a little bit about who wore it before me and what diseases they may have had. It was a quarter. I found a couple of other items I could use so I dropped about fifteen bucks total at the Thrifty 2ndHand Store. I also stopped off at a farm and ranch outlet and spent about forty bucks—cash.

I needed to satisfy my curiosity about something, so I drove another fifty miles or so south to the farmland my family used to live on. It was getting dark fast. Long November nights are kind of depressing, so I needed to hustle. For a moment, I thought maybe I had taken a wrong turn, but just as I was thinking about going back to the paved county road I had exited, I spotted it. It was still there. Our little pole shed that we always called the garage. But the barn that it used to sit near was gone. So was our house. Gone. No kitchen with the white metal cupboards where Mom would store the dishes. No kitchen table to eat breakfast at while Mom read the newspaper. No bedrooms. No furniture. Just plowed land where I used to give Golden a rub on the belly before I headed off to catch the school bus. The utility pole that served our farm with electricity was still there, about ten feet from the southwest corner of the garage. The building was covered with rusty tin and was big enough to hold about three cars, with a tall, slanted roof so you could park a high-profile piece of equipment under the tall part. As I got closer, I could see that the Jordans were using our garage—their garage—to shelter an implement.

I pulled right up to the garage, and there was a nice John Deere baler parked inside. I grabbed the old radio I purchased at the thrift shop in McPherson and uncoiled the cord. I walked to the corner of the garage and plugged it in. Ah, the sound of AM static. Just what I wanted to hear: the old garage still had electricity. I looked around, trying to see if there was anything there I would need to be aware of. There were a few old, square bales stacked to one side of the garage. The small bales were old, as that was a round baler parked there. It looked like they almost never frequented this place. Why would they? Their last cutting and baling of hay would have been a number of weeks ago. This place was several miles out of the way of their day-to-day operations. This would work perfectly for my "headquarters."

I had to get back to Salina for my final preparations.

TUESDAY

I went into the shoe store for my typical morning set-up procedures at 9:30 a.m. and got a big surprise. The front check-out counter was decorated with helium balloons and crepe paper. A computer-created dot matrix sign said, "Congratulations Joel," and another one said, "Best Wishes." David must have gotten the word out to most of the other store managers because, by about 9:40 a.m., there were at least a dozen other mall workers just hovering around in the shoe store, having a piece of cake and a cup of coffee. The mall opened at 10 a.m. for business, so it was a short sendoff, but it did make me feel good that my coworkers cared about my existence. Joy was there, even though she was scheduled off until after her baby arrived. I didn't have the nerve to ask her about the baby's father. I never saw her with a partner, but it was none of my business.

"Oh, heck yeah, Joel. I had to come to your party," Joy said.

One of the tellers from the bank was almost gushy. "Oh, I'm going to miss having you around, Joel. You are always so polite and funny when you come to the bank."

Thanks, and by the way, I'm fixin' to rob your bank in a few days, Jen. Oh, well, hopefully, she'd never find out.

A security guard swooped in for a piece of cake. I barely recognized him because he wasn't wearing his khaki mall security uniform, complete with radio, flashlight, and a huge ring of keys hanging off his belt.

"I've got late night tonight, but I wanted to say bom voyage." Yep, he pronounced the bon with an "m," like bomb.

"How late you gotta work tonight?" I asked.

"Last movie gets out at about midnight. I always hang right there at the exit." He puffed out his chest a bit. "Makes the ladies feel safe as they walk out to their cars."

"Oh, yeah?" I gave him a look, and he knew right where I was heading with my thoughts.

"Haven't got lucky yet." He had white frosting in his mustache. "One day I will. One day."

The best surprise came a couple of hours after the party when David said to me, "Well, Joel, why don't you just take the rest of today off and tomorrow too? You'll be working tons of hours in Hutchinson next week getting their new crew trained. I'll turn in the hours for you. Don't worry about it. We've got plenty of crew on hand."

Wow, these people treat me pretty darn good. Why am I leaving them?

Why did I always feel that my job helping people buy a pair of shoes was such a lowly position? Why couldn't I ever just tell people, "Heck yes, I work at that shoe store in the mall. I'm making the same money my ex-girlfriend is making teaching school. We have a great team of people. It's a good place"?

This freed up some time for me. It also changed some of the timeline of my planning. I went home shortly after noon and took a nap. I didn't mean to, it just sort of happened. Then, one of my roommates showed up with a couple of friends so I felt the need to be somewhere I could think. I walked to Coach's Sports Bar and sat on my usual bar stool.

"Opie, good to see you," said one of the regulars at the bar.

"I'd rather be seen than viewed," I recalled this old line a great uncle of mine would use. He lived out near the old farm, and I hadn't thought of him in years, but when I was there looking around at the old garage, I had flashbacks of him stopping by and giving me and my sister Marilyn a bottle of grape soda and telling us funny stories.

"Opie, is it true you're done at the shoe factory?" Petey seemed to always be on the leading edge of town news and happenings.

"Well, Alfalfa, it ain't a shoe *factory*, it's a shoe *store*, but yes, that's true. Today was my last day at the store here. I'm going to help train some rookies in Hutch starting on Black Friday." I was glad Alfalfa brought it up, as the three or four guys at the bar who all knew me now knew I'd be working in Hutchinson on Black Friday. Me working in Hutchinson on Black Friday was my alibi. The more people that knew I wasn't working in the Salina mall anymore, the better. Telling Petey this piece of news was probably as good as telling the local AM radio station. Petey talked to everyone.

I had exactly one beer and then walked home. That was Tuesday.

WEDNESDAY

I packed my bags for a weeklong trip. Tonight, I would leave Salina and drive to Mom's house in Kingman. I would enjoy her Thanksgiving meal, and then, on Black Friday I would be starting my stint in Hutchinson for seven or eight days. I could always take some laundry over to Mom's house if I got fed up with using the machines at the hotel. I gave my car a cursory inspection and noticed that one of my tires was extremely worn. Tire guys would say it was as bald as Mr. Clean's head. The last time I bought tires, I only purchased one—a typical cheapskate move. Now, here I was with one tire in good shape, two in fair condition, and one with bubbling sidewalls that were ready to give way at any moment. There was no way this worn-out relic would survive the number of miles I would be driving in the next couple of days, so I went to a local garage and bought the cheapest tire they had for $39, installed.

I packed the items I needed for the robbery in the trunk of my Volkswagen. I hadn't really thought much about it other than to stick to the plan, and if anything went wrong, even the slightest hiccup, I'd call it off and go back to my normal life until I got another chance to fulfill my purpose.

Since I was packed up, gassed up, and my tires were all good to go, there was only one thing left to do before leaving Salina and heading down to Mom's house in Kingman. Right before I walked out the door, I glanced across the room, and the message machine was blinking. No way! It surely couldn't be Nadine leaving me a message. This would change everything. I took a deep breath and pushed the Play button.

"Hey, Joel, it's David from the store. I meant to get you your Christmas bonus check yesterday at our little party, and it just slipped my mind. I will mail it to you with your paycheck if that's okay. If you need it sooner, you can come to the store any time before the next paycheck, and I'll give it to you. Take care, Joel."

I was relieved and saddened at the same time. Of course, I was hoping it was Nadine saying, "Hey Joel, come on up to Nebraska and move in with me, and there's some rich businessman who will hire you to take over his empire. In no time, we will have a house with a picket fence and a dog." But I was also glad that it wasn't Nadine because I had a plan, and for the first time, I was going to take charge of something and make a difference.

There was only one more thing to do as I left Salina. I drove the silver Volkswagen a few blocks and pulled over. I left the car running and walked half a block, peering down a dark street and waiting . . . for just the right moment.

I only waited about eight minutes—pretty good timing on my part.

I heard the door creak open and the same voice say, "There ya go, Ringo. Get out there and do your business, little buddy."

I walked up the street to the chain-link fence. I could hear Ringo prancing around, his tags jingling on the cool night.

"Hey, Ringo. Hiya, buddy," I whispered.

Ringo pranced up to the fence and smelled my fingers. The peanut butter did the trick, as he was immediately interested. I reached over the chain-link fence and down with my arm— basketball coaches always told me I should take advantage of my excessive wingspan—and I swooped little Ringo into my hand and stuffed him under my coat. He didn't make a peep. He kept licking my fingers until he got all the peanut butter off of them.

I felt bad about stealing—borrowing—Ringo. He was only going to be gone for a couple of days, and then he'd be back at home, but I knew his owner would be really upset. *I should have left a note or something*, I thought as I drove off, but that was an added risk I couldn't justify. Ringo and I headed the ninety-six miles from Salina to my boyhood home—well, the land that once contained my boyhood home.

When we got to the old garage, I could see that Ringo was a little uptight. I needed to get him to calm down; we had training to do. I opened the trunk of my VW, and the items I had purchased in McPherson were all just as I had left them. The first thing I did was get the mesh fencing out of the trunk of my car. I built a small four-foot by four-foot cage for Ringo to stay in. I plugged in a small electric space heater to warm the space a little bit. I placed it about three feet from the plastic mesh cage. I put the quilt in the cage for Ringo to have a bed. It was only going to get down to a low of 41, so Ringo would be safe.

I set up two bowls, one each for food and water, and put Ringo in the cage. I just sat down on a hay bale and hoped that Ringo would calm down a little. After about half an hour, I threaded Ringo into the harness leash I'd purchased at the farm supply store. The extra-extra small was the right size for sure. Now it was time to train Ringo and see if rat terriers were as smart as Greg Cooper, the critter extractor, said they were. I had snagged a money bag—the kind all the stores in the mall drop into the night deposit—from the shoe store. My goal was to get Ringo to bite down on the money bag.

I tried to get Ringo to bite on it by simply placing it in front of his face. No reaction. I had planned for this. Just like the guy at the wedding, his dog needed a scent. He'd had me spit on some socks. I grabbed a small bag out of the back seat of the VW that had dog treats and a few random items with which I would try to gain Ringo's interest. First, I tried sprinkling a little cinnamon on the bag and bingo! Ringo was interested. I gave him a treat. Now he was *very* interested. We made a little game of it. I was teasing Ringo with the cinnamon-scented bag, and Ringo was enjoying the game, and the treats. After I stacked a couple of hay bales, I held Ringo up about four feet in the air and lowered him to the bag, and when he bit on the bag, I pulled him up, got the bag, and gave Ringo a dog treat.

This was how I was going to rob the bank. At approximately midnight, I would approach the night deposit slot. I would sprinkle some cinnamon into the slot, thereby coating the bags that would have all been deposited a couple of hours earlier. I would squeeze Ringo into the slot and lower him to the pile of bags. He then would, hopefully, grab onto a bag. Then, I would lift him up, take the bag, give him a treat, and repeat. There would be at least twenty bags down there, with who knows how much cash. Very, very few people used plastic then, so the vast number of customers wrote checks or used cash.

So, it would be simple, right? Ringo just needed a little more training and things were looking good. I spent another hour training Ringo and then left him in the cage to spend the night in the garage. I went to Mom's house, about a fifteen-minute drive, and slept in my old bedroom.

THURSDAY, THANKSGIVING DAY, 1987

I woke up early in my old high school bedroom, got dressed, and was going to go check on Ringo. Mom was already up in the kitchen chopping onions and celery for her dressing. I would definitely be back for her Thanksgiving dressing with giblets—ooh-la-la, it is so good—after I checked on Ringo. After telling Mom I was just going on a short drive to see the old stomping grounds, I headed out toward the garage. I was a little worried that some pack of coyotes would dig under my makeshift cage and get to Ringo, and I was relieved when I got there to find that Ringo was fine. He had heard me coming from probably a mile away. He was actually happy to see me, reminding me of a joke that my redneck great uncle used to tell. "The difference between your wife and your dog is that if you lock both of them in the trunk of a car for an hour, when you open the trunk, only one of them will be happy to see you."

So, Ringo was happy to see me, and he was especially grateful for the deer jerky that I grabbed out of the fridge at Mom's house. A few more training runs with Ringo, and he was doing pretty well; he enjoyed the rewards, and he was really catching on quickly. Even though I assured him in my stupidest human-loves-dog voice that I would be back because he was a good boy, *such* a good boy, his eyes told me he was sad when I left him.

I got back to the house in Kingman, and Mom and Dad were working on the turkey dinner.

"Just got a call from Ross," Mom said. He was Marilyn's oldest. Ross and his sister Angela both had normal hearing. They would call my mom from the time they were little bitty kids and keep Mom up to date on how Marilyn and her family were doing. As the oldest child of deaf parents, Ross acted like he was twenty-one from the time he was about seven years old. "He said they are getting gas, and they are about an hour away." Mom was so happy that Marilyn and her family would be spending three days at home.

Believe it or not, I was able to have a very nice Thanksgiving, considering that my nerves were kicking into full speed off and on.

Dad and I did not share a single word with each other. We didn't share any turkey or even a glance either. We ignored each other pretty much like we had since I left home for college, except for the occasional sassy comments he gave me about college being a waste of money, and he'd often call after our defeats. If we won a game by a dozen points, never a peep. Get beat by twenty, and my phone would ring the next day. "Hey, son, how'd the game turn out last night?"

Dinner was actually nice. Mom told us about the books she had read, and also some current events that piqued her interest.

Ross and Angela told us all about school and how their dad's business was going. Ross had all kinds of stories about the jobs his dad performed and some of the crazy clients who hired him. Marilyn used sign language to set the record straight on a few of Ross's exaggerations.

Dinner ended about the time the Lions were probably losing another Thanksgiving Day football game, and I needed to get out and check on Ringo. I made up a lame excuse to cruise the country, but Ross, being a curious middle schooler, wanted to ride along with me. I walked him over to the laundry room and whispered, "I'm going to check in on an old girlfriend from high school, so you can't go with me, Ross."

He picked up on my vibe right away, gave me a nod, and a "good luck" grin.

I drove out to the old farm, and there was Ringo, happy to see me once again. We practiced a few "downzies" and "upzies" I would say as I was lowering or raising him back to approximately the height of the night deposit slot. About four times out of six, he'd grab the bag; he seemed to like the cinnamon I had sprinkled on the bag. The electric space heater was keeping the garage fairly warm, and I needed to get back to Mom's house.

"Take care, Ringo," I said. "I'll see you tomorrow."

One more instance of good luck came my way as I arrived back at Mom and Dad's house. As I walked into the front room, Marilyn's husband, Tomas, told me, using very elegant sign language, that I had a bad blinker light on my Volkswagen.

"It's a fuse," he let me know.

"Oh, shoot," I said. Because I thought that was a more appropriate thing to say than, *Holy crap, I'm robbing a bank tomorrow, and I don't need some cop pulling me over for a bad taillight and then shining the light on me until I confess to every crime since Nixon was president.*

"Wait a second, Tomas," I said out loud. "How can you tell? You weren't even behind my car."

Tomas read my lips expertly and responded in sign, "The reflection off the neighbor's truck. Your taillight is pulsing. It's just a fuse."

I could think of several times in the past when Marilyn's perceptions of various stimuli would stun us with their accuracy. We would typically think we had to explain things to Marilyn that she would interpret in a way that might be different, but it was Marilyn who made us look at things in a different way. It was like she had a different lens on the world that was a replacement for her hearing.

"Tomas can fix that for you, Joel," Marilyn signed.

"You mean like now? It's Thanksgiving night," I said.

"He's got everything in his tool kits, I guarantee it."

Sure enough, five minutes later, Tomas was digging into an extremely organized cabinet in the back of his van and locating a 10-amp fuse. I looked out in the driveway and could see him hunched down by the front door on the driver's side of my VW, locating a fuse box I didn't know existed. He quickly changed the fuse and issued a grin and a little nod as we verified that the problem had been fixed.

Tomas left me with one more laser-accurate prognosis.

"You sure are nervous about your upcoming job, Joel," he signed.

How could you know about THAT? I almost shouted.

Then it hit me that he was talking about my *insurance* job. I had not told the family that I was caught standing on the Unaware Fool Railway Tracks and got run over by the *Nepotism Express* heading full speed ahead to the Sanders Insurance Agency. There was no way I was going to ruin a family meal by dropping bad news like that, and the thought of Dad chiding me or pressing me for more details was the easiest way to ruin Mom's fantastic mashed potatoes.

"Yes, I am pretty nervous, Tomas," I signed the best I could.

"Don't worry," Tomas replied. "You'll be a total success, and you can take that to the bank!"

BLACK FRIDAY 1987

I woke up early at Mom and Dad's house, ate a Spartan breakfast, grabbed my bag, and headed north on state highway 14 to Hutchinson, Kansas. We weren't open until 10 a.m., but several stores were opening early, and the mall parking lot was already about three-fourths full. You could tell it was going to be a full day at the mall.

"A full day for sure," I muttered as I pictured myself opening a shoe store in the morning and robbing a bank by midnight.

Black Friday is a crazy day at the mall. The sheer volume of people makes every merchant feel like they are working on an assembly line. This makes for a great way to train employees. I could put one of the trainees on the register, and they would easily do as many transactions in one hour as they might in an entire shift on a random Wednesday. Same thing with fittings or replacing stock. We would have so many transactions going on that the two new manager trainees would be getting an onslaught of training that would take days and days to get in, say, October.

I did have one peculiar transaction where I made what could have been a mistake. Bruce, a district manager from one of the clothing stores, came over and said, "Hey, Joel, I see they got you in Hutch now. Did they move you up to DM?"

"No, I'm just helping train for a few days," I really didn't want to give him any more info than necessary.

"Can I write you a check for a hundred?" he asked.

I had done this occasionally for him in Salina, and he had done the same for me. It looks bad for a manager to write checks to his or her own store and cash them, so we helped each other out from time to time.

But for some reason, I told Bruce, "I better not. I can't risk running low on cash today for the drawers."

I had plenty of cash in the store safe, but my brain was confused. I was stammering around because I was thinking, *If I cash some check, then the FBI comes across it and ties me to the crime.* Heck, I was in Hutchinson! The bank I was going to rob after closing time was in Salina. Anyway, confusion and paranoia had a hold of me, and those two fellas can twist a guy's normal, logical brain into a mind full of fuzzy guesswork. I stood my ground. Bruce would have to get his cash from the bank like everyone else did.

Damn. Sigmund Freud was right. I remember talking about this in a psychology class, how your subconscious can just quickly take over an action or thought, causing you to make an illogical decision. I didn't want to leave some "clue" but here I was, behaving in a manner unlike I normally would—thereby leaving an actual clue. Bruce kind of gave me a strange look like, *Well, okay, dude, I hope you never ask me for a favor.*

I was able to calm myself well enough to function throughout the afternoon. Being mega-busy all day really helped with the whole anxiety thing. I'm not a tremendously nervous person, but when it's time for the big game, I get a little nervous. I was at the shoe store until a little past five. Skip had been trying to shoo me out the door since about four. "You have to open tomorrow and work all day Sunday, go get some rest. Go enjoy the good life at the Hampton."

"Yeah, you're right, Skip. I better get my rest. It's a big weekend," I said gratefully.

He had no idea.

I drove over to the Hampton Inn and checked in. Skip had everything in order. All I had to do was sign on the dotted line. The process only took a couple of minutes, but I hung around in the lobby and talked to both the folks working the desk and another worker who, by the look of his uniform, appeared to be their maintenance man. I wanted these folks to know that I was here . . . and when I was here.

"Well, Black Friday really brought out the crowds to the mall," I said.

"Oh, I bet," one guy at the desk said. "I don't even fight those crowds."

The other one said, "I was there among the masses. I love it. My sisters and I got some great deals early this morning."

"Have a good stay with us, Mr. Howard."

And just then, a new Christmas song came on the piped-in music of the hotel lobby.

"It's Joel," I said. "Joel, just like in this song." I pointed both index fingers in the air and tilted my head.

They listened for a second, then laughed, and then we all sang along with the famous Christmas carol.

"Jo-el, Jo-el, the angels did say."

CHAPTER SIXTEEN
PERFECT

Len Barker was a major league baseball pitcher. Anyone that makes a major league team for even one game is a very, very good baseball player. According to the numbers, Len Barker's performance was about as average as you could possibly be in major league baseball. As a pitcher, he won seventy-four games and lost seventy-six games in his career. But one night, against the Toronto Blue Jays in 1981, Len Barker pitched a perfect game. Perfect. Twenty-seven batters faced and Len Barker got all twenty-seven out. Not one man reached first base. Not a hit, not a walk, not an error, not even a hit batsman. At the time, it was only the tenth game in the history of baseball, about 112 years, to be a perfect game. In 112 years, with thousands of games played each year, it's mind-boggling that a pitcher seen as average among his peers would accomplish perfection.

It's an achievement that can be equaled but can never be bested. Barker undoubtedly pitched on teams with pitchers who were far more successful than he. He shared the field with All-Stars and faced Hall of Famers. But on that one night, this so-called average pitcher had his night. Nine innings pitched, not one batter could claim victory. Len Barker had his perfect game.

After Len Barker's perfect game, after all the celebrating, one of the local TV stations in Cleveland thought it would be a great idea to call Len Barker's grandmother and tell her that her grandson had pitched a perfect game.

She said, "Oh, tell him that's great, and I hope he does even better next time."

CHAPTER SEVENTEEN
THE HEIST

I unpacked my bags, putting my clothes into the drawers and closet since I was going to be there for several days. I called the desk and asked for a 7 a.m. wake-up call. I exited the Hampton Inn using a side door so the front desk staff wouldn't see me leave. It only took about half an hour to drive from the Hampton Inn down to the farm to get Ringo. It was dark and pretty darn chilly, and I was concerned that Ringo would be stressed, or worse.

Once again, there was Ringo, happy to see me. I put him in my warm car, and I could tell right away that he was appreciative. He gave me a look that said, *Are we going to play the bag game?* and I promised him in my stupid human-dog voice that, yes, we were going to play the bag game because he was such a good boy, a good boy indeed.

Then I froze. Headlights. Approaching from a little less than a mile away, I could see headlights. It was damp enough tonight that there was very little dust trailing the car. As the vehicle got a little closer, I could see that it was a pickup truck. The only people who use these roads are neighbors. Most likely, if they saw a strange vehicle on their little country road, they would stop to ask if you needed help. If you needed help, they would likely get it for you, but what they were really asking was, *Why are you here? That's the Jordan's hay baler sitting in there, and you dang sure better not be tampering with it!*

This was the country, and that truck would have a weapon in it.

I sat in the driver's seat with a lot of possible scenarios going through my mind. Ringo even looked a little worried to give me some sympathy.

The one thing I kept repeating in my mind, *If ONE thing gets thrown off the plan, that's it. It's canceled.*

The pickup, a real old beater, slowed down and then sped off when they saw a car parked in the garage. I could see it was two kids. The long-haired blonde scooted over so close to the driver that his snap-back cap was almost pushed against the driver's side window. From the looks of things, they had plans for the garage tonight, and now they were off to find another place out in the middle of nowhere to have some private time.

"Dang," I said out loud to myself. "I didn't think about coming out here during high school. This would have been way better than over by the oil rig that always put off a weird odor."

I waited a couple of minutes, but they weren't turning around, so I carefully put the garage back like it was. I put the wire mesh cage, the quilt, and the space heater in the trunk of my car. I had four-plus hours to kill, and I had to make sure no one saw me or the cute little dog that I had dog-napped. Too bad there were no drive-in movies in the winter, that would have worked. The park really isn't the place to hang out for more than ten minutes when it's 21 degrees outside. Parking in the middle of nowhere wouldn't work because one "helpful" farmer coming by would ruin the whole plan. I couldn't take Ringo back to my place in Salina. Nobody could see me in Salina.

I wound up driving about halfway to Salina and pulling in at a rest stop off the interstate. I figured the only people who might see me or Ringo here would be traveling. They would be long gone tomorrow when the bankers showed up and found a dog inside the vault where the cash bags should have been.

When 11:30 p.m. finally arrived, I put the old Volkswagen on the path to either a job accomplished or a real messy life. Right as I merged onto the highway, a car came up behind me. The car stayed behind me for about a mile, and I knew it just had to be a cop. Who else would be out on the road late at night on a holiday weekend? I was thanking Tomas with every breath for fixing my taillight. But what if he didn't get it fixed correctly? What if it was pulsing again? *The cops are somehow onto me . . .* then my brain, the logical side of it anyway, took over and reminded me that driving down a highway is not illegal and there was no way any cop would know that I was on the way to rob a bank in Salina, even if my taillight was pulsing.

Five minutes later, the car eased around me. Not a cop. My paranoia was able to take a short break.

I wanted to arrive right at midnight, and sure enough, the bank clock turned to 11:59 p.m. right as I entered the mall parking lot. That's not uncommon in rural Kansas. We can always guess within a few minutes how long it's going to take to get from one city to the next. You'll never hear someone around here say, "It will depend on the traffic," when judging how long a trip will take.

I had a mental vision of the security guard, far out of sight on the opposite side of the mall. I was 100 percent sure he was there just hoping a lonely lady would desire to be walked to her car. Maybe tonight would be the night he got lucky. There were a few other cars in the lot. I parked near the bank.

I grabbed the small stepstool, my large army-style duffle bag, and the star of the show, Ringo. I double-checked one jacket pocket for the cinnamon and a pair of scissors; the other pocket had my pull-down winter mask and gloves—and treats for Ringo. I put the gloves and mask on, which really didn't look suspicious because the temperature was dropping quickly. I did not walk directly to the bank door. I went about twenty-five yards south of the bank door and then edged along the outside of the mall, my body pressed against the outer brick wall, my face looking out toward the parking lot.

Not a moving car or person in sight. I quickly stooped down in a low crawl, scrambling quickly to the deposit slot. I placed the stepstool directly under the slot and told Ringo, "All right, buddy, let's go."

As I stood up quickly on the stepstool while holding Ringo in one hand, I had a flashback to the "photo of the week."

One of the security guards had come around several weeks ago showing all the managers at the mall. "Hey, guys. Look here. I got the photo of the week." He showed us some grainy pictures of . . . of . . . well, it looked like an elbow and a wrist maybe. I knew exactly what it was. It was the young girl trying to reach into the deposit slot when she dropped her bracelet. The camera, which is about two inches above the deposit slot, showed her elbow and her neck. It was not in focus at all due to how close she was to the camera.

I stood on the second step of my two-dollar stepstool, confident that the camera would only show my chest. They would see the most popular winter coat in Kansas. They might see an out-of-focus Ringo going down the slot. That would be about it.

I almost forgot the cinnamon because I was in such a hurry to squish Ringo through the slot. But luckily, I remembered just in time and sprinkled a generous amount of the spice in the slot. Then came the moments of truth:

Would Ringo fit into and through the slot?

Would Ringo grab a bag?

Could I pull him up and then extricate the bag from Ringo's jaws?

I had to turn his head to the side a little, but he went right down the slot with no trouble. Ringo grabbed a bag. I easily pulled him up by the harness. He gave me the bag and wanted to play the game like a golden retriever playing fetch with his favorite tennis ball. About every third bag, I would give Ringo a treat. My duffle bag was filling up with cash bags. A few minutes passed, and Ringo was getting exhausted. It seemed that maybe all the bags were gone.

It was a little difficult to maneuver since I had to stay so close to the camera directly above the drop slot. There was no way I could get Ringo back through the deposit slot, and I had known this all along. I took the scissors out of my pocket and cut the leash. Ringo jingled to the floor. His tag on his collar would have him back with his owner in a matter of hours. I opened the deposit slot one last time to check on Ringo. I could hear his little claws prancing on the expensive, newly polished granite floor of the bank. I could hear the jingle of his dog tag, and I could faintly smell the cinnamon I'd sprinkled down the shoot.

I hopped off the stepstool, crouched as low and close to the building as I could, and got around the corner with all the speed I could muster to get out of the view of the camera. I pulled out of the mall parking lot with a huge duffle bag full of money bags and a stepstool in the trunk of my car. I drove a couple of blocks and turned into a Burger King parking lot. They were closed, but my gloves, mask, coat, scissors, and the remainder of Ringo's leash went down deep into their trash receptacle. I put on the coat I'd had for a few years and aimed the VW toward the Hampton Inn on the north side of Hutchinson.

On the drive back down to Hutchinson, my right leg was about to fall asleep. As I wriggled in my seat a little, I discovered why. I had shoved the can of cinnamon into my right hip pocket and I had been sitting on it, causing the nerves in my leg to send out waves. I pulled it out of my pants pocket, spilling it all over my center console, fingers, and pants. Oh well, I like the smell of cinnamon.

Just as I was about to exit the highway to pull into the city of

Hutchinson, a car came up pretty quickly behind me. My heart started pumping a zillion beats per minute. If it was a cop behind me, this could really end badly. I had to turn on my right turn signal and also tap my brakes. If that taillight that Tomas fixed wasn't working correctly, I was going to need a story for why I was out at 1:30 a.m. in the morning and why my heart was beating loud enough to be heard a mile away. At least, it seemed that was the case.

The car eased on past me as I slowed to turn. I don't think it was a police car, but I kept my eyes straight on the road as to look disinterested and innocent of stealing a bunch of cash bags from the night deposit at some bank sixty miles north.

When I parked my car at the hotel, I looked back on my day. Every part of the plan had gone perfectly. It was perfect. I had my Len Barker moment. Perfection.

Remember now, there wasn't really much luck involved yet. This was all just a matter of making a plan and carrying out that plan. The luck was on its way, though, and it was headed straight for me.

CHAPTER EIGHTEEN
POST HEIST

I arrived back at the Hampton Inn and used my plastic slide card to go in a side entrance. I walked down the hall carrying my huge green army duffle bag. I thought about leaving it in the trunk of my car, but every once in a while, you'd open up the morning paper and read about a rash of car break-ins. Stadiums and hotel parking lots are prime for that type of looting. I didn't want to look out my window in the morning and see my trunk lid popped and the contents missing. I had some plans to secure the money.

As I walked into the elevator, I could not believe the feelings that came over me. The adrenaline was coursing through my body like crazy. At a cellular level, the insides of my body were firing off synapses faster than lightning bolts. I couldn't wait to get into my room and start separating the cash from the checks. I was like a kid on Christmas morning, tearing open the biggest gift under the tree. How much cash would there be? The checks were worthless to me, of course, and I was going to mail them back to the bank. At least, that was the original plan. The more I thought about it, the more I decided that that was an opportunity to mess up. So, the checks were going to be torn into minute pieces soon and discarded, never to be seen again. How was I ever going to get any sleep? I had to work at the shoe store in Hutchinson all day in a matter of hours. My mind was whirring like the fast-forward button on a VCR was glued down.

Just after I pushed 3 on the elevator and the doors began to close, a shape came around the corner, sticking a hand in to catch the elevator. The door opened wide, and in walked a woman—a woman of maybe thirty years of age. The first thing I noticed was that she was wearing a lanyard around her neck, some sort of identification badge. The next thing I noticed was that she was attractive. *Very* attractive. About five foot eight. Auburn hair. Some freckles. Did I mention attractive? Really pretty auburn hair. Eyes to match the hair, they were golden.

Then she spoke.

"You travel in the old style, eh soldier?" She shifted her gaze toward my big circa-1960s army duffle bag.

Did I mention her auburn hair and the way it matched her freckles, eyes, cheekbones, and smile and that she had a very nice physique? Brick HOUSE. Oh, man!

I don't know much about biology and pheromones and hormones and stuff like that, but this girl was working my shit. I had the euphoria of the money bags, and then standing there in front of me was this . . . well . . . Just the way she stood there. One foot slightly in front of the other. Tilting her head just a little and looking into my eyes. Receiving my eyes with hers. The way she smiled. I think the motion of the elevator going up added to the whole aura. She wasn't resisting my obvious interest. Man, the adrenaline that was bubbling like crazy was now moving into a whole other sphere of human sensation. Like a Super Bowl of sensation.

I wished the hotel had one hundred fifty floors and that we were riding the elevator all the way to the top.

She held her badge up diagonally, with her thumb and index

finger, and said, "Dental hygienist seminar. Gotta get those CEUs."

She wasn't wearing a wedding ring.

The elevator came to a stop, and the door opened. We both walked down the hallway, and I couldn't keep myself from walking closer than the norms that usually govern strangers in public walkways allowed. She wasn't shying away. If anything, she was welcoming the closeness. Her elbow bumped into my hip. She tilted a look up toward me. I said something dumb about the weather. "The old mercury really dipped tonight, didn't it?"

I got to my room, and when I stopped at the door, Miss Gorgeous Auburn Hair stopped, and I could tell she was going to say something. I opened the door only a little way and looked back at those eyes. I welcomed her, stepping just barely across the threshold. I opened the door a little wider. If I had had one of those neon signs businesses have in their windows, I would have pulled the chain to make it declare OPEN.

Then she said something that shot my adrenaline clear past the top of Mount Everest.

"I want to stick my tongue in your mouth."

I carefully placed the duffle bag in the corner of the room, placed the Do Not Disturb sign on the door handle, and shut and locked the door behind us, and, oh my, oh my.

I was no romantic pro, but my gosh, I have to say, my performance was All-Conference or maybe even All-American. She and I were a perfect fit. When I first kissed her, I felt like I was on the other side of her. She just melted in my presence. She knew how to make her mouth feel like something . . . well, she knew how to make a kiss feel like *way* more than a kiss.

So Len Barker's grandma was right; there are things better than perfection. What an unbelievable night.

We were . . . active—very active—for over an hour and then fell asleep. I had called for a 7 a.m. wake-up call. I had no idea when I requested that wake-up call that I would spend the night with Miss Passionate.

When I awoke, it was still dark. I reached across the bed, and she was gone. *Wow, she was quiet. I never heard a thing.* Then, I freaked out! I threw back the covers and jumped out of bed. *Oh shit, shit, shit. Oh my God, what if she took the duffle bag?*

CHAPTER NINETEEN
AFTER THE AFFAIRS

Debra Miller hung up the phone and stared at her brothers. "Well, that was another creditor. Dad had liens all over town. We are going to have to sell off all his stuff, guys."

The boys knew this was the way it would have to be.

"Would have been nice to spend Thanksgiving together one more time," one of the brothers said. "From now on, every year around Thanksgiving is gonna be pretty tough."

"We are setting the funeral clear back to next Friday. I have my hands full with a million little details, so we need to stall. Dad's affairs are such a mess," Debra said.

Her choice of the word "affairs" made both brothers look up from their crossed fingers over their own bellies that they had been staring at. One son and one daughter from each marriage. Both marriages fell victim to Joe's lifestyle, and as Debra had said, his affairs were such a mess, which was true in every sense of the word.

"Guys, let's try to sell as much stuff as we can by then. I'll get the titles to the trucks, and I will ask around at all the banks," she said.

"So, ya just gonna sell the truck Dad just died in Debra?"

"Yes," she said defiantly.

"Like, today?"

"I hope so. And, as I was saying, I gotta go all over town seeing where he had bank accounts. Maybe he had multiple accounts. I know he always thought he had to hide money from our moms. You two get the choice task of selling the guns, that four-wheeler, and all of those hideous deer heads if you can. The sooner we can get Dad's . . . umm . . . money situation in order, the sooner we can all get past it," Debra said in an all-business tone.

CHAPTER TWENTY
SURPRISE!

Just as she had been doing every working morning for the nine months the mall had been open, Janice Stevenson turned her key to open the back entrance to Bank IV at the Salina, Kansas, branch. She immediately turned up her nose. What was that smell? It was so foreign.

"Good Lord," Janice said out loud. "It smells like dog poop in here."

Twenty minutes later, at least five cops and a dozen bank employees were gathered around.

"How did they do that?" was the line that kept being repeated.

According to the *Salina Journal,* the next day, numerous cash bags and an undisclosed amount of money were missing, and detectives were following several leads. Police were confident the money would be recovered and anyone involved in the theft would be brought to justice in a swift manner. Crimestoppers was going to announce a significant reward for anyone who would come forward with information leading to an arrest and successful prosecution.

CHAPTER TWENTY-ONE
THE ROOKIE

LeeAnn Schiebler had two major emotions concerning her first solo shift on the Salina Police Force. For four-plus months, she'd been in the company of four different partners, and now she had the A shift all by herself. A Saturday morning patrol. *This should be a nice, calm morning.* Maybe a few tickets for illegal left turns or a roll-through at a stop sign. Drive past some bar parking lots and see how many people left their cars and got a friend to drive them home on a drunken Black Friday night. *Calm, nice, and calm.* Her first emotion was a deep feeling of accomplishment. Not just because, in 1987, she was one of the first policewomen on the force in Salina, it was about completing a program. That feeling of a summit summited. No one could say she wasn't made of the right stuff. Of course, emotion number two was kicking in pretty strong too, and in the words of LeeAnn, she was "scared shitless."

It was less than half an hour into the shift when she heard the scanner screeching like a pack of hungry coyotes about the robbery at the bank. Tidbits about the night deposit drop box, a small dog, and she thought someone said cinnamon.

If I robbed a bank, what am I doing next? I've got a bunch of money, sure, but I might have some physical evidence I need to unload. Where would I dump it?

LeeAnn was on the fifth trash can she had checked in the area, this one at Burger King, when she hit the jackpot. A blue coat, a pair of gloves, a ski mask, a pair of scissors, and a portion of a dog leash.

She froze. *I gotta be careful here.* She knotted the top of the plastic bag, placed it back in its container, and yellow-taped the trash can with a six-foot perimeter. LeeAnn then had a flood of memories hit her from her training. Well, not her training exactly, but her first few weeks on the job, when it seemed every single thing she did was scrutinized and criticized to the nth degree. The chain of command told her to notify her sergeant. She needed to do it in a way that didn't alert any of the lurkers who liked to comment on her performance. Their comments were never positive. The lurkers had convinced LeeAnn she'd never make it through two weeks of training post-academy. They'd put a live raccoon in her squad car and dog poop in her locker. They would shake their heads with a dismissive posture when she asked a question, and they would never give her credit for being correct when she offered solutions. Their end result was that every decision she made was full of self-doubt and scenarios replaying in her mind like Super Bowl highlights. She found herself checking and re-checking herself on the most mundane tasks. *Did I lock that door? Did I turn off my radio? Did I store my weapon correctly?* LeeAnn had never been a self-doubter, but then she'd never had a group of haters watching her every move, hoping she'd make a critical error and be dismissed from the force. A whole barrel of good apples can be tainted by one or two bad ones—at least, that's what Michael Jackson used to say.

LeeAnn radioed the precinct and asked to speak to her sergeant.

"Hey, Sergeant Buckley, could you meet me at the Burger King, the one out south, past the mall?" LeAnn asked.

Buckley was back with, "Sure thing, Officer."

The fact that he kept it professional was soothing to her. From others, she'd been called "kiddo" and "young lady," and one jackass had chimed in with " Hey, Charlie's angel."

"Hey, Sergeant," LeeAnn said quickly before disconnecting. "Bring that new video camera with you if you can get your hands on it."

Just as Sergeant Buckley was rolling up to Burger King about ten minutes after LeeAnn called, the strangest thought hit her: *Why in the world would Burger King be using cinnamon?*

CHAPTER TWENTY-TWO
PERSON OF INTEREST

The two cops got into their squad car after leaving Carlos Villa's house on Saturday just before noon. "That was one happy pup," the tall one behind the wheel said.

"So, you think Villa has *any* involvement at all?" his partner asked.

"Ah, hell no," the tall cop said. "Did you see how happy he was to get his dog back? That was the only thing on his mind. All we got from the photos is that this guy is like six foot eight! Maybe taller."

"And the army duffel bag, at least that's what it looked like to me."

The tall cop shook that remark off. "Did you see that limp? Looks like Villa's got arthritis something terrible. Our guy was in and out of there in eight minutes. There's no way Villa could have walked around the building where there is no camera in twenty minutes! But the clincher in mind—guilty guys don't invite cops in to play games with their pets."

"Well, I'm glad ol' Rusty—"

"Ringo, pretty sure he said, Ringo," corrected the tall one.

"Yeah, that's it, Ringo. Glad he's home. We are going to have to write a very detailed report on this," the short one reasoned.

"Exactly! This is the kind of report that can get you a promotion. This is the type of case where Crowder will be looking at *everything* we do. Every note we take, every report we file. We are getting every single word right. Straight to the station, even though I'd kind of like to swoop through for some McD's coffee."

"You know how that ends up," the short one said. "We're liable to see something going on, and then if we stop and deal with that shit, our report will be all garbled."

"We ain't taking no chances—straight to the shop." And with that, the two cops headed directly to the station, used the back entrance to keep from being distracted by the usual bullpen banter, and filled out their report. In that report, both cops stated that Ringo's owner was definitely *not* a suspect.

About an hour later that night, Captain Dean Crowder read their report. He then called the police station in Garden City, Kansas. After a brief exchange with a dispatcher, Crowder was able to talk with a patrol officer.

"We have a Carlos Villa up here in Salina, and according to the DMV, he lived in Garden City until recently. Have you guys ever had any dealings with this individual?" the captain asked.

"We've got a ton of Villas here, Captain, but I'm pretty sure I know Carlos and his twin brother, Roberto. Those two were really good wrestlers. Now, Roberto has had a few run-ins with some folks from time to time, but as far as I know, none of the other boys—and there's about five or six of 'em—none of them ever got in trouble. Every one of 'em's a heckuva wrestler, I'll tell ya that," the officer answered.

"That one that got into a little trouble, what kind of crimes we talkin'?"

"Nothing major, Captain," the Garden City officer said as he thumbed through some paperwork. "Just a minor burglary when he got mixed up with a crooked construction outfit."

"What's this Mr. Villa doing now?" Captain Crowder wanted to know.

"Get this: he's got a dog grooming business. I know because my wife takes our two pups to him. He's doing good now. You can't believe how much money people are willing to spend on their dogs."

"Dog grooming business," Crowder said. "I'm sure you're right. Big dogs, little dogs, I bet he's good with 'em all."

"I'm sure he is. Some people are just animal people. He probably works with cats and birds and anything else people call pets. Hey, Captain, if you want me to put out a BOLO on Roberto, I could do that, and you could talk to him over the phone."

"Aw, I appreciate that, but you don't have to do that just yet," Crowder said.

After five minutes of chit-chat, he thanked the officer for the information and went to the filing desk, where he found a folder neatly placed in a basket. Crowder then changed the report to say that Carlos Villa was a "person of interest." Captain Dean Crowder then took it upon himself to begin investigating Carlos Villa.

CHAPTER TWENTY-THREE
BO JACKSON

I ran to the corner of the hotel room with the most dreadful thought of finding my army bag gone and a thank you note in its place. I fumbled for the light. Not finding it, I dropped to the floor and felt around with my hands.

The duffle bag was still there, thank God. After successfully turning on the light, I pulled back the outer flap, and apparently, it had not been disturbed. The cash bags with the Bank IV logo printed on them were neatly tucked inside my big army duffle. I quickly dug through the bag and to my great relief, she had not taken any of the loot. I folded the outer flap over the duffle, closed the curtain, and sat down on the ottoman in the corner of the room, and a flood of tears ran out of my eyes. I just bawled. I had no control over it. I wasn't sad. I wasn't happy. I've cried sad tears. I know all about 'em. I was still having a few bouts of sadness over Nadine that would strike at the most random of times. And I've cried happy tears too. When we qualified for state basketball during my junior year of high school, the tears just leaped right out of those little tear ducts that usually hold 'em back. So, I don't know what type of tears these were. But they were flowing. It took me a good two minutes to calm my breathing. I looked down and my underwear was around one ankle. *Oh. Last night.* No tears there. Holy cow. I had a vision of that auburn hair. That body. Those freckles. *Did that really happen?*

Then my nickname for her hit me. Sorry, but that's the way my brain works. Her nickname would be Bo Jackson. It was easy: Bo Jackson was the greatest player ever for Auburn University—football, baseball, amazing athlete—and that auburn hair and "greatest ever" was working in my mind in tandem, and that's why I would always think of her as Bo Jackson.

My night with Bo Jackson was sort of like playing golf alone on a deserted golf course and getting a hole-in-one. There was no one to witness it. Anyone you told would question it. *Was it really a hole-in-one? Did you use a mulligan? Come on, what are the odds? And what about Bo Jackson? A dental hygienist seminar? On Black Friday? Who schedules seminars on holidays?*

Had I just hallucinated the whole thing? One look in the full-length mirror at the Hampton Inn and the intense hickey she left me right below my right nipple erased any doubts about it being a product of my imagination. *Wow. She was real. Real amazing.*

Would I ever see Bo Jackson again? I didn't know. What would I say if I did? What if she saw me enter the hotel after 2 a.m. and told certain people? People that are good at putting two and two together? What if the cops came around asking people . . . Then I calmed down a little. The bank is in Salina. I was in Hutchinson. Sixty miles away and safe as . . . money in a bank. There would be no reason for them to worry about me, as I had worked all day on Black Friday at the Hutchinson store. *Calm down. Calm down.* Obviously, she never looked inside the duffel bag or that cash would have been gone for good.

I needed to get cleaned up and get to work. I was on four hours of sleep, at best, and I was going to be working a long day at the shoe store. After a shower, I put my coat on and grabbed the army bag. I opened the duffle to double-check that all the bags were really inside. There were at least twenty bags in there! Most of them were the simple zip-up type. Some of them were a strong fabric and had a large zipper with a lock on them. I would need to get a good pair of tin snips to open those bags.

I shoved the duffle bag into the bottom dresser drawer, made sure the Do Not Disturb sign was still hanging from the door so no one would enter while I was gone, fiddled with the door to make sure it was really locked, and headed to the lobby. I made sure to tell the staff hello and thanked them for the free breakfast.

"Y'all need anything at the mall? I'm gonna be there all day," I joked.

"Sure, here's my Christmas list," was one reply from the desk.

"I saw a nice Jeep parked in there," was the other.

———

TRAINING at the store was going well. The two new hires were eager to get Skip and me out of their hair so they could manage the store. They were plenty capable and experienced, so I had no doubt the store would do well under their management. As long as I was busy in the store, my mind was cruising along on autopilot pretty well. But, when I would take a short break to just sit with my thoughts or stroll through the mall, my mind would crash into paranoia land. I didn't pay attention well enough in psychology class to know that meant my mind would be going one hundred miles an hour concocting schemes that ended with me in a whole lot of trouble with the law, which led to the visions of me in prison, where my mind was especially creative and cruel. A gauntlet of dozens of angry men who were skilled with aggressive gestures, chants, and physical torture.

As I walked through the mall in the late afternoon, I

happened upon a small, seasonal kiosk that had a variety of hand tools. They had some really interesting gadgets and tools. There were displays of battery-powered screwdrivers and novel household items that would end up in crowded kitchen junk drawers all over Kansas. I came across a decent pair of tin snips, so I dug into my funds and purchased the pair. I was fairly certain they were tough enough to penetrate the reinforced fabric money bags, but just in case, I also bought a utility knife with a razor blade. That should be able to pierce the fabric, and the tin snips could take it from there.

As the transaction was almost complete, I had the urge to scream *NO!* and run down the mall, jump into my car, drive to Mom's house, and erase the entire robbery from my mind. But no, I had to calm myself and finish the plan. Not an easy thing to do. Throughout the next few days, while I was trying to teach about inventories, stocking, displaying, and ordering, my mind was on the money. Well, the bags. I hadn't actually seen the money yet. For some reason, I wasn't ready to look inside the bags. After work, I'd pull the army duffle onto the bed and just stare at it. I guess the joke was on me if there was no money in those cash bags. Bags full of notes that read, "Ha, ha, Joel. We got ya!" My mind was going bonkers. *Of course, there's money in those bags. They're money bags. They hold money. They aren't prank bags to play pranks on bank robbers—bank robbers? What?* My mind spent another ten minutes tossing that around, and my thoughts circled back to the aggressive convicts and their welcoming chants for me at their super-max prison.

On Saturday, after closing, I walked down to the bank deposit with one of the trainees. The night deposit slot at the Hutchinson bank was of a different design. You'd place the bag on this roller—it reminded me of the tracks on an army tank—push a lever, and the bag rolled in on the rubber roller and dropped into the bank. The slot was only about three inches tall.

No way I could get Ringo through that slot or back out. I wondered how long until the Salina bank changed their deposit drop into one of these.

I thought I better give Mom a call, just to let her know I was okay and how much I appreciated her Thanksgiving dinner. I wasn't sure if I would tell her about the insurance job falling through the cracks, but I probably wouldn't until I had some type of good news to offset the bad.

"Hey, Joel, thanks for calling," she said warmly.

"You beat me to it, Mom. I called to thank you."

We were only on the phone for a couple of minutes, but her voice was always calming.

"You know Joel, your dad is very proud of you," she said.

I just mumbled, "Oh, okay," because *Mom, that's the stupidest sentence you've ever allowed to formulate in your brain* was way too harsh for my sensitive and caring mother.

"He always wished he could have gone to college, but he didn't want to ask his folks for any financial support. With your dad, it was baseball. He wanted to play baseball so bad in college. He played a lot of town team ball, but that wasn't serious enough for him. He ached to go to college. But we got married, and Marilyn came along soon after. It was a different time, Joel. You're fortunate that you got to go."

I had never heard about any of this stuff, and I didn't know what to say. I couldn't really interrupt with, *Well, Mom, I just robbed a bank, so I'll have plenty of money, but I must be getting on with my life.*

To tell you the truth, the only thing that popped into my mind was *I wish Nee Nee was here to talk about this. She would be able to provide just the right advice.* Dang. I missed her.

On Saturday and Sunday, I took a couple of empty shoe boxes to the hotel with me. Sunday night, I double-checked that the Do Not Disturb sign was still on my door—where it had been since my night with Bo Jackson. I methodically began inspecting the money for the first time. It seemed like it had been two weeks since Ringo handed me that last bag and I cut his leash. It had been just under forty-eight hours.

As I was opening the duffle, if I noticed even the faintest of sounds in the hallway, I would freeze and think the cops were going to start banging on my door. Then, I would wonder if maybe I heard light footsteps in the hallway. *Could that be Bo Jackson?* What would I do if Bo Jackson showed up?

I could smell the cinnamon when I opened the duffle bag. To this day, I still get a pretty strong blast of memories any time I get a whiff of cinnamon.

After getting my breathing under control, I went through all the easy-to-open zipper bags. The check-to-cash ratio was a little disappointing. The amounts of the checks were staggering in some cases. Two hundred, three hundred, and five hundred dollar checks add up to some pretty big money. I recognized some names on some of the checks. Coach B spent a couple of hundred bucks at JCPenney. My roommate spent some money at Waldenbooks. The training I got from David at Kinney Shoes was trying to convince me I should make neat, straight columns and catalog exactly how many checks and the exact amounts. The logical side of my brain won that argument quickly, so I took the checks, and instead of carefully tabulating each and every one, I tore the checks into tiny pieces. I put the pieces into a McDonald's sack that held my supper only a half hour earlier.

I figured nobody would be surprised to see a person at a hotel throwing a McDonald's sack into a trash can. I felt relieved when the McDonald's bag left my hand and fell deep into the trash receptacle in the breezeway at the Hampton Inn. *Now there's no physical evidence, proven evidence, to find in my possession.*

I went back upstairs, and then it was time to count the cash. Now, the accounting side of the brain won out. I made a nice ledger out of the stationery the hotel provided. I took the bags out of the duffel. *Ahhhhh* . . . I would have to get rid of the bags, every one of them, before I could claim that there was no physical evidence that could be connected to me.

The tin snips required some effort to cut through the reinforced fabric. They actually worked pretty well for a while. Then, I started to see why they sold them so cheaply at that mall kiosk. The tinsnips were beginning to lose their tension. I still had about ten bags left, and these cheap cutters weren't going to make it. So, I started cutting a hole large enough to drag the cash and checks out. By the last bag, those tin snips were wobbly and had become noodle snips, maybe, at best. I finagled them the best I could. It was a workout. My wrists and fingers were sore, and my forehead was covered in sweat, but I got every bag open.

I'd brought a large black trash bag to the hotel from the shoe store, and I placed all the bank bags in it, compressing it down to a size that would easily fit under my arm. I would toss that bag into the large dumpster near the back entrance at the mall.

Now it was time to count the cash.

Number of bags: twenty-three. Wow, Ringo was amazing. He snagged twenty-three bags in about three minutes. That's eight bags a minute. What a champ!

Largest amount of cash in one bag: $37,241, from Dillard's. The movie theater came in second place at $29,387.

Smallest amount came from a kiosk that sold sunglasses: $81.

Most of the bags had between $3,000 and $8,000 cash in them. The Salina Mall is pretty small in the grand scheme of things. In fact, it's probably one of the smallest malls in America. I could only imagine how much money got deposited at the mega-malls all over the country on Black Friday.

The cash would not fit into two shoeboxes like I thought it

would. Instead, I used my suitcase and one shoebox. I made two trips down to my car. As quickly as I could without drawing attention to myself, I put the money in the trunk of my VW Golf, which, unlike most Volkswagens, was in the rear of the car. Then I parked my car right by the front door of the Hampton Inn, in the most brightly lit spot I could find.

CHAPTER TWENTY-FOUR
HARASSMENT

Captain Dean Crowder banged on the door on Monarch Street until Carlos Villa stood up out of his recliner, limped across the room, scooped up Ringo, and said, "I'm coming. I'm coming."

"Hello, Mr. Villa, is it okay if I come in?" Crowder said as he wedged the door open and walked right in.

Carlos was a little shocked that the officer just barged in like he did, but he had to either back up a few steps or get his bare feet stepped on.

"Do you speak Mexican or American?" Crowder asked, still advancing into Villa's front room of his nine-hundred-square-foot house.

"I speak English just fine," Carlos said proudly.

"Good, cuz I'm here to find out what you know about your dog and the bank job. And don't act like you don't know what I'm talking about."

Villa wanted to tell him that the cops had already talked to him, but he figured that sounded like what a guilty person might say. He started to speak, "Wha—"

Crowder interrupted, "What I want to know is how did you train that dog there to fetch a bank bag? Who helped you drop him in the slot? Most importantly, where's the money, Sane-yore Villa?" he asked mockingly.

Crowder walked right past Carlos into the kitchen. It was a small galley kitchen, and except for a dirty pizza pan on the stove, the space was very tidy. Crowder opened up a couple of cabinets until he opened the one he wanted. It had a spice rack hanging on the inside of the door. He peered intently at the spices, then picked up a small can of cinnamon, "Is this the one ya used, Hay-zoos?"

"It's Carlos, sir."

"I know," Crowder said. "I just think it's funny you people name your kids Jesus." (This time he used the Gee-zus pronunciation.) "Just trying to be supportive of all my Chicano friends out here in the world."

He shook the spice can.

"So, did ya use this one, or did your *amigo* bring the cinnamon? Oops, Not *amigo*, that means friend. Your *hermano*, isn't that the word for brother?" the captain said derisively.

Mr. Villa had no idea what he was talking about.

"Sir, two officers were already here earlier," he said.

"Those two?" Crowder chortled. "They couldn't pour piss out of a boot if the directions were written on the heel. I'm leaving now, *señor*. But, I'm making more phone calls—especially to Garden City. You got a brother out there, right? He still locked up? Or is he out now? He good with dogs or something? Did they teach him all about dog handling in the joint? I've heard of them classes. Cons are gettin' all kinds of edjumacation these days. If you decide you need to talk, ya know, make things easier on yourself. I'm pretty sure *you* know how this game is played . . . come down and see me. Bring the cinnamon again."

With that, he chuckled and walked out the back door. Crowder walked the perimeter of the small backyard, checking the chain link fence for openings. He also tested the latch on the gate. Then he walked out the gate, left it swinging open, and strutted around to his police car, marked, and drove off.

Carlos Villa didn't know whether to be more nervous or furious. The remarks about his brother were so rude. Ringo could tell his human was upset, so he dashed across the room and skidded to a stop on the hardwood floor, grabbed a stuffed toy in his teeth, and goaded Carlos into a game of tug-of-war between friends.

CHAPTER TWENTY-FIVE
FUNERAL ARRANGEMENTS

"Jesus Christ, Debra, for once will you just believe us? We sold all the guns to the guy, who I admit *is* a rip-off artist, but nobody else wants to buy a bunch of random, somewhat crappy, no paperwork guns," Joe Miller's oldest son pleaded with his determined sister.

"You guys could have gotten more if you would have just tried a little harder." And with that being said, Debra's body language softened a little.

She added, "Dad would laugh at us right now, wouldn't he?"

The younger son's eyes were a little watery. "He'd say, 'She's on this earth to keep you two knuckleheads in order!'"

The three offspring of Joe Miller shared a quiet laugh.

"Do you think, um . . ." the younger brother nervously approached Debra.

"There's no way she will show her face," Debra said about her half-sister. "The funeral starts at two. Be at the church by one-thirty . . . and don't wear a stupid hat. And no jeans. Well, nice jeans would be okay."

The brothers nodded in submission like little bear cubs who had just been corrected by a mama bear.

CHAPTER TWENTY-SIX
NO GOING BACK

I was breaking down some cardboard boxes in the backroom of the Hutchinson, Kansas, shoe store, when my district manager came walking in with his spiral planner in hand. "Joel, these guys got this place moving along the tracks pretty well," Skip said. "So, I'm outta here today. I need you to put in one more day tomorrow, and then these birds can fly the coop, or however that goes."

I didn't want to tell the boss that I thought he had his nests and coops mixed up. And, to tell you the truth, I was secretly hoping I would have two or three more days at the very most left on this Hutchinson Mall assignment.

It meant I didn't have a job after tomorrow at about three o'clock, but there was a way bigger picture than that for me. I just wasn't happy. Not even a little bit. I had money to live on for quite a while, but really, I had nothing to look forward to. I couldn't ever go back to Salina. I didn't want to live around Mom and Dad's place. I was starting all over with no friends, no place to live, no schedule, and no direction.

When I went to college, I already knew a couple of other kids at the school, and I had a team. A team is a tribe of built-in friends. I had guys I spent every afternoon with—we were always either working hard toward a common goal or just goofing off.

Now, I had nothing.

That afternoon at the Hutchinson shoe store, I asked a couple of customers who were about my age if there was a good sports bar in town. "You know, somewhere I can watch a game, have a beer—someplace quiet."

They both told me about a place on the south edge of town. It had a funny name: Suds in the House, or maybe it was House of Suds.

"I like it," I said. It had been a while since my neck and shoulders were not tensed up against my paranoid plotlines bouncing around inside me. I even had a relaxed grin on my face.

CHAPTER TWENTY-SEVEN
IN THE HOUSE

I walked into House of Suds, or as the regulars called it, "the House," and in less than three minutes, I felt like I'd found my vibe. By today's standards, big-screen TVs back then had horrific, grainy pictures, but in 1987, that big screen was a thing of beauty. There was some soft music playing, almost no smoke present, and a big, U-shaped, arching bar that allowed patrons to talk to each other. I had thought about how I was going to respond if anyone asked me if I was new around here.

It didn't take long.

"Well, I'm trying to get a job over at the junior college," seemed to be a good enough answer, and the questioner went right back to his chips and beer.

I limited myself to two quick beers and barely entered a conversation about the NFL season. I knew I had to work one more day at the shoe store, and then my future was totally up in the air.

Where would I go? What would I do? I had a trunk full of cash and I had absolutely no idea what the next forty-eight hours held, let alone my future.

CHAPTER TWENTY-EIGHT
THE FUNERAL

J oe Miller's funeral didn't last even fifteen minutes. It would have been less, but his daughter Debra, looking at her watch, said, "Give her two more minutes. Then we go. I knew she wouldn't be here," talking about her half-sister she had not seen for about ten years.

There was no music, and the minister of the small country church where Joe's parents had been long-time parishioners had little to say. He asked if any of the dozen or so in attendance would like to speak. Debra came forward.

"Dad's favorite prank was when he sold Shorty Riggs that old Chevy Blazer a few years back . . . Well, Dad always hid a key in the rear wheel well in one of those magnetic key boxes. Every vehicle he ever owned. So, any time he'd see the old Blazer parked downtown, he'd move it a few spaces. Or, to the other side of the street, and then he'd wait about half a block away to watch Shorty look for his car. I think Shorty's Blazer gave out about a month before Dad's heart did. Several of his other pranks we probably couldn't discuss in a church."

The minister tried to comfort those gathered by saying Joe would be resting next to his parents in the graveyard just out the east door of the church. He made them feel even more comforted by only evangelizing for five minutes, maybe less.

CHAPTER TWENTY-NINE
ALL THAT DOUGH

It had been four or five days since the robbery, and Brad Phillips was self-talking himself into a state of indignation. "Dang, I could have gotten away with a good one," he'd mutter to himself while he was in the back room at Sbarro, grating mozzarella cheese or rolling dough into five-inch balls that would make seventeen-inch pizza crusts.

"That dang Jim got my mind rolling, and now I can't turn it off," Phillips said right out loud to himself while he was getting the pizza place ready to open. Jim was a manager at Foot Locker who had popped in right before close on Monday after the robbery.

"Well, I'm kicking myself," Jim said to Brad as he was grabbing a late-night slice of pepperoni and sausage.

"Why's that, Jimbo?" Brad asked.

"Black Friday, I had a drawer that was thirteen bucks short. I just tossed in the thirteen bucks to even it out so I wouldn't have to fill out a dang shortage form and hear 'yak, yak, yak' from my district manager. So whoever robbed the dang bank got away with my thirteen bucks. Bank has insurance. Foot Locker will end up with *my* thirteen bucks! Pisses me off."

Never mind that Foot Locker got Jim's thirteen bucks either

way, but that got Brad Phillips thinking about all the deposit bags that were stolen on Black Friday. The robbery was consuming his every thought. At the close of business on Black Friday, Brad was so exhausted that he hadn't followed the normal procedure of filling out the deposit and walking it through the mall to the night deposit like almost every other business in the mall had. He had started to, and he had two bags that day, about four grand, all cash. But, by the time he locked up, counted the drawer, and made out the deposit slips and a change order, he was just too tired, too physically drained. All he could think about was heading to his small apartment, turning on some CMT, and falling asleep to the music channel's country hits before having to get up early on Saturday morning to put in another long day at the pizza place. He knew it would be a busy day on Saturday. The mall would be crawling with lots of shoppers and moviegoers wanting something to eat that wasn't turkey.

"Screw it. I need the sleep," the Sbarro manager had said. "I'll drop it in the morning. I have to open this place and get to be here all day tomorrow too."

So, Phillips had just left the deposit bags in his car overnight. Early the next morning, Brad would be opening the store for "Pizza Saturday," one of the biggest days of the year in the pizza business. He drove to work, parked near the mall bank, and walked up to the bank deposit slot. Instantly, Brad Phillips's internal radar was telling him something was wrong. As he pulled down on the handle of the hinged door of the deposit slot, he noticed several things.

1. There were a bunch of people in the bank: *What the heck? The bank doesn't open for two hours.* He saw a cop, Janice the bank lady, and several people he didn't recognize.

2. A guy was holding a dog—a little bitty dog. *In a bank, what the heck?*

3. Three or four uniformed cops were now in sight coming from the other direction.

4. As he dropped his deposit bags down the slot, a strange sensation hit him. "Why do I smell cinnamon?"

Of course, the word got out, and by about two o'clock that day, Brad heard the bank had been robbed. And that was what was bugging him.

If I wouldn't have dropped those bags, that money would be mine! They would just assume I deposited last night like I always do. Shee-it. Cash. All cash because of Sbarro's pain-in-the-ass policy that we can't take checks. Oh, man, all that cash could have been mine.

His mind had become possessed and obsessed with the thoughts of what four thousand bucks could have bought. With that money, within weeks, he would have been moving back to Oklahoma. Sbarro wouldn't be hurting. The bank insurance would pay the exact amount like Jim from Foot Locker had said. He had a carbon copy of the deposit slip; it would have been the easiest heist ever.

Dang. I knew stuff was weird that day. I almost just kept walking and didn't stop at the bank. I could have just kept the bags! They would never know. That dog? Hardly a dog. More like a large rodent. I like a good-sized, medium to large dog. Like an Australian shepherd or a Labrador retriever to take pheasant hunting. When I get my own place, that's what I'll get me. Right when I smelled that cinnamon, I almost clung onto those bags and just headed down to the store until I figured out what was going on. Dang, four thousand bucks! It would have been like a bonus. And the way they keep changing the bonus plan, they kind of owe it to me anyway.

Brad's thoughts would ramble on for most of the morning while he worked to get the pizza place up and ready for another day of business. He even went back and looked at the copy of the deposit slip. There it was in duplicate: $4,021.76 and a $350 change order. The adding machine on his tiny desk quickly told him he had just let $4,371.76 slip out of his grasp.

The phone rang, and it was a pay phone. The Sbarro corporate office in New York didn't want employees talking on the phone during work, so when employees needed to make a call, they used a pay phone. The manager had a code to dial when they needed to contact the home office, and that was the only outgoing call that was supposed to be made. After all, you were supposed to be making and selling pizza every minute on the job.

"Sbarro in the Salina Mall, this is Brad. How can I help you?"

"Hey Brad, it's Lane in Hutchinson. How you doin'?"

"Oh hey, Lane. I'm good. Did you hear the bank here in our mall got robbed?"

"No way!"

They chatted about that a bit, and then Lane got to why he had called.

"I need a couple cases of sausage to get me by until the next truck. If you could spare it. I could meet you halfway."

"I'm good for sausage, no problem. I tell ya what, Lane, I'll just head on down this afternoon. I need to get out of here for a while. Maybe I'll catch a movie at your mall or something. I need a break. I've been going nonstop all week, getting ready for this weekend. My assistant manager is here till close, and I finally have plenty of staff. I could leave here about one thirty, after the lunch rush dies down. Will that work for ya?"

"Heck yes," Lane said, happy to have a missing item on the way soon. "Are you sure you can break away?"

"Yep. No problem, I've got the whole crew working. I'll see you in a few hours."

"Thanks a ton, Brad," Lane said.

The whole sixty-mile drive down to Hutchinson, Brad just couldn't quit thinking about those four thousand dollars. Instead of being able to set it off to the side and think, *Oh that's ridiculous. You wouldn't really try to steal the money,* he began to heat up in a roiling anger.

After dropping off the sausage and some straws, Brad asked Lane if he wanted to go get a cold one.

"I can't this time, but thanks," Lane said, trying to end the conversation so he could get back to work.

"If I had all my gear with me, I'd run out to some of those wetlands and get me a goose or two right before sunset, but heck, I can't really wade out in these, can I?" Brad held up his foot to show a pair of common brown penny loafers. He even had a nice shiny penny in the slot above the arch of the foot on both feet.

The two just gave a short chuckle, thinking about trying to hunt in wetlands with a pair of loafers for footgear.

"See ya next time, Lane." Brad headed down the corridor of the mall. He skipped the movie he had considered catching and decided to hit a little bar and grill he'd popped into one time on the south edge of Hutch. He thought it was called Suds R Us or something catchy.

Ten minutes and only one wrong turn later, Brad saw the sign for House of Suds. "Ah, there it is! House of Suds. Hmm. I like 'Suds R Us' better."

Brad entered the cozy joint, and it was just as he remembered it: some big screens for sports, no loud music blaring, medium lighting (so you could see who you were talking to), bowls of peanuts, and very little smoke. As he strolled toward the bar, he thought he saw a familiar face. Here he was in Hutchinson, but he was pretty sure he knew that face from the Salina Mall.

That's the shoe guy.

CHAPTER THIRTY
BRAD'S IN DEEP

"This is Sbarro's in the Hutch Mall. How can I help you?" Lane answered the phone as he peered out the back room of the pizza place, hoping the people at the counter were getting served with a minimal wait.

"Hey Lane, I'm sorry to bug you," a young male voice came on the other end of the line. "This is DJ, the assistant manager in Salina. I really, really need to talk to Brad, um, Phillips. Our manager. He said he was running some stuff down to you. Sbarro's regional manager is here! He heard about the robbery, and he wants to talk to Brad like right now!"

"Sorry, man, you just missed him. He left like fifteen minutes ago," Lane said.

"Did he say where he was going? I'm afraid he's in deep shit the way they're talking." DJ was clearly panicking.

Lane thought a second. "I mean, it's a long shot, but he might be at the House of Suds right now, just having a beer or watching some college football. He told me he likes that place."

"Okay. Thanks, Lane. If I hear anything about these guys heading your way, I'll let you know. They got me on pins and needles right now."

DJ then walked up to the front of the pizza place and told the regional president what he had learned.

"Thanks. You get up there and sell pizza. I'll try to get a hold of him at this Suds place. By the way, your line looks good. You make those sausage rolls?"

"Yes, sir." DJ swallowed hard, trying to regain his cool.

"Keep it up. Your egg wash on the dough is just the right consistency." He turned to the pay phone, pulled a plastic phone card out of his pocket, and feverishly began punching numbers.

"Operator, connect me with the House of Suds in Hutchinson, Kansas, please."

CHAPTER THIRTY-ONE
RESTING PLACE

George Collins was catching a little nap with his feet up on a well-worn desk in the graveyard shed he called his supply hut. George had dug graves for three rural church graveyards in Reno County, Kansas, for over twenty-five years. This particular graveyard was his favorite because he had this nice little hut. It had a comfortable chair, the kind that had wheels, and you could lean way back, raise your feet up, and get a proper nap. It was shaping up to be a colder than average autumn, and the ground was firming up with each day as the sun set earlier and crossed the skies lower. Those ever-lengthening shadows were a sure sign that winter was right on time again. When George had a helper, they could dig a grave in about three to four hours. On a solo job, which he'd been doing a lot lately, it could take him a full day, and maybe he'd have to finish up in an hour or two the next day. George had cut it close with Joe Miller's grave, finishing it up only about three hours before the funeral.

This nap is gonna feel good, George thought to himself as he covered himself up with a heavy wool blanket and clicked on a small space heater. George snoozed throughout the graveyard service, which amounted to little more than the minister offering one short prayer and Joe's sons cranking the casket down and tossing on one shovel of dirt each in a solemn moment.

The solemnity lasted only a few moments actually, as the boys could be heard laughing about a private joke on their way down the sidewalk back to the little country church where their trucks were parked. Except for George's old sedan, the parking lot was clear in a matter of minutes.

CHAPTER THIRTY-TWO
A MESSAGE

I gave my goodbye handshakes to the new managers at Kinney Shoes in Hutchinson, Kansas, and walked out of the mall a lonely guy. I had no job. I had no home, really. I mean, my stuff was back at the triplex house in Salina, but I couldn't live there again. I wasn't going to go stay with my parents; the daily chirping from my dad would cause me to grab an icepick and stick it through my eyeballs.

I did have my '83 Volkswagen Golf with a trunk full of cash. Not many people could say that, I figured, so at least there was that one positive.

I remember walking to my car and thinking, *If this was a movie, Bo Jackson would be in the front seat of the VW, fanning out a handful of bills, saying, "Jump in, babe. Let's go to Canada."*

I got to the car and found I wasn't in a movie. In fact, a little puddle under the VW made me worry that maybe I had a gas leak. That's all I needed was some absent-minded smoker throwing a smoldering cigarette butt under my car, and the thing bursts into flames! To the firemen trying to put it out, it would just be a cheap car on fire. Only I would know that that trunk contained over $138,000 in cash. I backed out and eyed the puddle. It looked like old oil that had probably been in that parking lot for weeks. Paranoia was thriving in my mind like algae in a warm Kansas pond. Every passing car was an unmarked cop car. Every ringing phone was an undercover agent reporting my whereabouts. An airplane innocently flying over-head would make my heart jump and my breath catch. I decided I'd drive over to the House of Suds and try to relax a little. There might be some college football games on the tube. The Miami Hurricanes were undefeated, and I was hoping to catch a little of their game to see if anyone could pull off an upset against them. I needed something normal to occupy my out-of-control oscillating brain.

When I pulled up to the House of Suds, I noticed the place was super quiet. Only three or four other guys were at the U-shaped bar, and maybe a few couples were scattered at the tables across the bar. I noticed there was a pay phone booth across the way, so I figured now would be a good time to do something I'd been putting off for three or four days.

I called my house in Salina, and one of my roommates, Clint, picked up and accepted the collect charges. He knew I was good for it. Clint and I always split our bills out fair and square. I had a couple of other roommates who had tried to skate out on a phone charge, utilities, or even rent when they were moving out.

"Hey, Clint. It's Joel. What's up?"

"Hi, Joel. Not much. You still down in Hutch?"

"Yes, but I'm done here now, not really sure what's next for me. Might take a few days off . . . I gotta find a job," I said.

"Job? What about the insurance agency?" Clint asked, sounding concerned

"That's a long story, man. I'll tell ya about it sometime," I said, secretly thinking in my mind that I never wanted to speak about that episode of utter disappointment again to anyone, anytime.

"Well, hey, Joel, I'm glad you called cuz I got a message on the machine I want to play for you," Clint said.

My heart skipped a little. There was only one voice I wanted to hear on that message machine. Then the paranoia interrupted, and I was freaking out, thinking I would hear something like, *This is Officer Buzzkill from the Salina Police Department, and you, Mr. Joel Howard, are going to prison for a good long time.*

"I'll try to get this to play out loud. I listened to it cuz I didn't know who it was for," Clint said. "If you get cut off, just call me right back."

Clint must have hit the right button because I'll never forget what I heard on that machine.

"Hey, Joel, it's, um, Nadine. How ya doin'? I'm not trying to be super weird here or anything, but I've been thinking about you lately, and I wanted to visit with you. I'm really happy up here in Nebraska . . . and . . . Anyway, this might sound weird, but you'd like it too. I have a cool group of friends that I teach with. We play cards. We play basketball and volleyball in the school gym late at night. Anyway . . . Oh, and one of the guys is a boss at some grain company, and they need to hire someone. And for some reason, as he was talking about it, the job duties, etcetera, I thought, *Joel would love it here. Joel could do that job.* It's a mid-management thing. Oh . . . and I have a guy that I'm . . . well, I'm *with* a guy. So, I'm trying not to be weird, cuz that's all good, but I'm just trying to be a friend. Weird message I know . . . Anyway, my number is 308-555-2094. Call me if you want. Bye."

Wow. Holy crap! Nadine! A job! Friends! Are you kidding? This was amazing. I mean, super weird because Nadine was with another guy, but a job and friends and things to do . . . it all sounded pretty good. *Maybe things wouldn't work out with Nadine and this guy.* No, that wasn't where my brain was. This was an opportunity that could get me on track to a productive life in a new place with no worries of the past bumping into me. I would need to take this opportunity before I got "Skinny Sandersoned" again, and this guy who has a job hires his brother or cousin or whatever. This was the green light in life I was waiting for, and I needed to step on the gas. I walked out of the phone booth and over to the bar.

"Dang. You look happy. Did they hire you over at the JUCO? You gonna be a Blue Dragon?" asked Robert Clemons, the owner, who had apparently overheard my conversation from last time.

"Oh," I kind of stammered as several fellas around the bar waited for my answer. "Not yet, for sure, but it looks good. Thanks."

While they raised their glasses for me, my mind was rapidly producing a checklist. I needed to get my stuff out of Salina, settle up with Clint on the house bills, and head to Nebraska as fast as I could. I needed to mail my forwarding address—after I had one—to the shoe store so I could get my last paychecks. And I needed to call Mom and tell her I was moving up north.

I was staring at the bubbles of carbonation rising up in my draft beer when I thought I heard my name. My mind had to shift gears from the checklist it was cranking out and actually listen.

"Joel? Hey, you're the shoe guy. From Salina. How's it goin'?" It was Brad, the Sbarro manager—from the Salina mall.

What the heck is he doing here?

CHAPTER THIRTY-THREE
THE SCOOP

Police Captain Dean Crowder was ready to put his plan into motion, so he made a phone call to Garry Grant, a rookie reporter for the *Salina Journal*.

"*Journal*. Garry Grant speaking."

"Garry, this is Captain Crowder with SPD. How are you doing this fine day?"

"Oh, I guess I'm doing fine, sir. What can I do for you?"

"I've been reading your stuff, Garry. I like your style. I have something for you, but I can't quite go on the record yet, if you know what I mean."

Garry quickly grabbed a brand-new steno notebook, the kind that are about the size of a half a piece of paper with the wire spiral across the top, and a blue Bic pen he trusted. He was buzzing at the prospect of a police officer offering him a scoop.

Before he could even ask him what it concerned, Crowder said, "It's about the bank job. The robbery on Black Friday."

Holy cow! Garry's mind was tossing him questions faster than he could say them. Five minutes later, the reporter had what he considered a major front-page scoop. If only his editor could let him run with it, this would be the kind of byline that he could bank on for years to come. His string book, a journalist's collection of stories, would now have a legitimate front page. The night when the drunken grandma had shown up at the city rec department meeting would have to move back exactly one page.

CHAPTER THIRTY-FOUR
DISASTER PREPAREDNESS

Joel Howard's paranoia was shifting into overdrive, and he was thinking maybe he was on the edge of pure hallucinations. *Why the heck would the pizza guy from Salina be in this random bar in Hutchinson?* was the only cogent thought Joel could come up with. His mind was throwing so many strands of delusional doom at him that he felt like a kernel of popcorn dancing inside one of those huge popcorn machines at a movie theater. The hair on the back of Joel's neck stood straight at attention as he remembered his college friend saying, "That guy's a twisted dude," after a job interview at the Sbarro pizza place.

"Joel? Hey, you're the shoe guy. From Salina. How's it goin'?" pizza guy said, taking a stool across the U bar from him.

"Yeah . . . Um . . . how ya doin'?" Joel stammered.

"Well, I just swapped out some stuff with—"

And at that moment, pizza guy was interrupted by the loud voice of the bartender, who had a phone in one hand and a bar towel in the other. "Is there a Brad Phillips here? Brad Phillips."

Brad and Joel both just kind of looked at each other, surprised.

Brad pushed his stool back and started moving toward the phone, "Yeah . . . that's me."

The bartender invited him through the swinging section of the bar that employees use to get from behind the bar out to their table. Brad answered the phone skeptically, "This is Brad."

It was the regional manager of Sbarro who had flown to Kansas from Pennsylvania. He had already conducted a couple of interviews with the bank, and they let him see footage of the deposit box from Friday night. He now had one thing on his mind.

He introduced himself with all the proper corporate office talk and titles, but Brad's mind was quickly doing the interpretation. This was an oh shit guy, maybe the biggest of the oh shit guys! After introducing himself, he got right to the point. "Brad, I have spoken with the bank and also audited the store in Salina. You did not deposit the Black Friday receipts until 8:02 a.m. *the next day*. That was 8:02 *Saturday* morning. I found some other small violations in the store, but suffice it to say, missing a deposit is a firing offense. You have been fired from the Salina store. You don't need to turn in your keys. I am having the locks changed as we speak. Your last check will be mailed to the address we have on file. Do you have any questions?"

Brad was stunned.

"Fired?" he stammered. "Missing? No way! I deposited every penny. I only didn't do it that night because I had worked from 7:30 a.m. to 9:30 p.m. on Black Friday. We beat the forecast by twenty percent. I was short-staffed on Friday night. I've put in over sixty hours every week this month."

"I'd say that goes to your inability to manage your store correctly. We thank you for your previous efforts. Do not attempt to enter the store. That's all I have. Thank you, and good day."

Brad Phillips, now an ex-pizza guy, hung the phone up and half walked, half stumbled through the back room to where he'd just been sitting at the bar.

"Three and a half years for that company, waiting to get a

decent store out of this shithole state, and now they dump me over nothing," he muttered to himself.

One of the patrons at the bar noticed Brad's obvious change in demeanor and said, "Well, cowboy, it looks like she just called ya after putting all your stuff in the front yard."

"And set it afire," said another. The laughter was light. They wanted to know the story before they let go with all-out laughter.

Joel also noticed the dip in Brad's demeanor and was hoping it would spur Brad to leave and go back to Salina. Joel didn't need any hiccups in his plan to get to Nebraska and get on with his new life.

It was said under his breath, but Joel clearly heard Brad when he muttered, "Jesus. Can't believe they fired me."

And just then, an earthquake hit.

Not the kind that shakes the earth, although Hutchinson, Kansas, does get an occasional earthquake. The earthquakes in central Kansas usually register around three or four on the Richter scale. This one didn't shake the earth; it shook Joel Howard.

It shook him good because a beautiful woman with auburn hair walked out of the backroom of the House of Suds. Bo Jackson. She, with that beautiful hair, face, and body, walked right through the swinging door in the bar. She looked like she was heading out to clean off tables or take some orders. She was wearing jeans and a brown T-shirt with the company logo: an image of a house with a topped-off beer mug where the front door should have been. Bo Jackson stopped when she saw Joel Howard and looked directly at him. She put an ordering pad down on the bar and lightly dried her hands with the towel draped over her shoulder. She stepped a few feet closer to Joel.

The earthquake in Joel was shaking him at about 7.5 on the Richter scale, and it was headed for an earth-shattering 10.0.

"Hey, Cinnamon," Bo Jackson said, clearly within earshot of

several patrons of the House. A big smile bubbled up on that gorgeous face. "I haven't seen you since you fucked the daylights out of me on Black Friday. Oh my, the Hampton Inn. We had an amazing night, didn't we?"

Joel's insides were curdling, and he felt his face go every color of red. Nee Nee's paper was right. Every red blood cell in his entire body was headed straight for his neck and face. He had no control over this reaction, and his brain had no answer for the automatic response that was making his face as hot as the grill beyond the swinging doors in the House of Suds.

"I've never been with a man who put cinnamon on his fingers," she said. "But I liked it. It was fun licking that cinnamon off your fingers. It wasn't the only thing I licked . . ."

Just then, one of the patrons swung down quickly off his stool and positioned himself halfway between the gorgeous waitress and Joel. He quickly interrupted, "Molly. Now, Molly, that is very rude. You need to apologize to this young man and go back to the kitchen and help your dad out back there."

"But it's true," Molly said. "We had a wonderful night. I'll never forget it cuz it was Black Friday. I hope you call me some-time . . . *Cinnamon*. Or I could call you *Money Bags*." Her beautiful eyes were staring straight at Joel as she gave him a grin, shrugged one shoulder up a little, and turned to go about her business.

The bar patron lightly touched Molly on the arm. "You need to go to the backroom, Molly. Come on."

And then, quick as a snake, Molly jerked away from the man and started cursing at him. It was an entirely different voice, and her visage changed so much that it was like she was playing a different role in some community theater production. Her actions then went from community theater to local hospital psych ward as she grabbed a hunk of her own hair and pulled it hard. She pulled out a fistful of that beautiful auburn hair, embedding her fingernails alongside her face as she did.

That beautiful, angelic face. Blood started to trickle down her cheek. Molly was guided to the back room, letting out a string of curse words until the swinging kitchen door closed behind her.

Joel Howard and Brad Phillips were both shocked, but the other patrons at the bar had a look about them that made one think they had seen similar outbursts from Molly before.

"She's like, schizo," one customer said, shaking his head.

Another one said, "Technically, it's not schizophrenia. That's the term everyone uses, but she's more like multiple personality disorder or something. She's like that movie *Cybill* that was on TV a few years ago with Sally Field. Sometimes she says she's a church secretary, and sometimes she says she's a nympho-dental hygienist. She also plays a veterinarian and an art teacher from Paris."

"Plays?" one of the regulars said, "she ain't playing. It's not some traveling circus act or amateur theater. That's just who she is that day."

That educated sentiment drew some odd looks from most of the fellas at the bar.

Looking directly at the two newcomers to the bar, the guy with all the information went on with his lecture. "Yeah, okay, fair enough. Anyway, her dad, Robert, owns this place, so she helps him out some, and most of the time, she's fine. Robert and his wife adopted her from like Romania, or somewhere. They adopted her when she was an infant, but they didn't get her out of there until she was like four years old, so it's been a rough go for them. She's made claims like that about other guys in town, even a preacher."

"And a married woman," added another customer with an incredulous grin.

"She don't mean no harm," one of the regulars said to Joel. "But it's best to handle it just like you did there. You just gotta let her be Molly . . . or whoever she's bein' that day."

"Yeah, one night, a guy tried to play along with her, and let's just say he found out Molly's dad is left-handed."

"I saw that guy downtown six days later, and he still had a black eye."

Joel thanked the patrons for their support and started to excuse himself. As he was rising to go, he looked across the way and saw Brad, but not in the way he had seen him just a minute ago. Earlier, Brad had the typical surprised expression that one might have when running into a colleague who worked in the same mall in some small bar sixty miles away. Now, Brad was staring at him, examining him, like he was a big ol' Colorado spotted brown trout in a fish tank of nothing else but little bitty Walmart goldfish.

Joel's paranoia kicked up, and he broke eye contact immediately, but he could still feel Brad's eyes—his penetrating, scrutinizing eye—on him as he said a quick goodbye and headed out the door of the House of Suds.

Whew. You talk about luck. None of those guys in there believed one word she said or asked any questions. Cinnamon? Money bags? They thought she just made that up out of the blue. His hands were shaky as he tried to get his key out of his pocket to unlock the VW. Joel Howard had to calm the earthquake and get on his way to Nebraska.

CHAPTER THIRTY-FIVE
JOURNO 101

"I know you don't want to name your source, Garry, but you have to tell me," the managing editor of the *Salina Journal* told his rookie reporter. "I will not betray your trust, but we can't run it if I don't deem it a credible source. That's the standard, Garry. Good grief, that's Journo 101. We have to be responsible."

After nodding his head and considering his options—name the source to his editor or miss out on the scoop—Garry Grant told his boss, "It's Captain Crowder . . . from the SPD."

"All right then, Garry. Good job. We'll run it. Call him 'a ranking officer on the police force.' I want to see the copy at least thirty minutes before first deadline."

CHAPTER THIRTY-SIX
I HEAR YA BOGEY

Well, cross House of Suds off my list of places I could comfortably hang out at. As you might imagine, I hustled out to my VW to get away from that scene. I felt bad for Bo Jackson—Molly. She was struggling with things in her past that made her life difficult. Sheesh, I had to get out of there. I was reviewing my mental checklist just as I was opening my car door.

"Hey, wait up."

It was Brad—the pizza guy, well, ex-pizza guy from Salina. This was the last guy I wanted to talk to. In fact, I didn't want to see or talk to anyone that had anything to do with a mall, a bank, a shoe store, a pizza place, nobody. I just wanted out of this whole scene.

His Ford Bronco II was parked two slots down from mine, and he opened his car door real quick and then closed it. He came around the back side of his Bronco, and his stride was weird. He was holding something just off his hip to hide it from me.

He came up to the passenger side of my VW.

He had a gun.

A freaking gun! A black and silver handgun.

What the hell is this guy doing?

"Get in and start your car. Turn on the heater. I'm freezing," the maniac said.

He pointed the gun at me, and he was trembling a little. I don't know if it was from the cold temperature or his nerves. Either way, I did not feel safe. Not 1 percent of me felt safe. He got right to the point.

"I know you did the bank job. Where's the money?" Brad growled.

I tried to look clueless.

"Cinnamon?" he said.

I'm pretty sure my clueless look turned into a scared-as-shit look. I was experiencing the exact opposite of blushing. My face was white as a piece of typing paper because I could, no exaggeration here, feel the blood draining straight down out of every extremity and somehow forming a ball of emptiness in my stomach like I'd never experienced before.

"Your last day in Salina was Black Friday," Brad said. Truly, he was off by two days, but when a guy is holding a gun aimed at you and his hand is shaking like a bass on a stainless-steel hook, you tend to leave those minor corrections alone. At least I did in this case.

"I don't know how you did it, but I have enough facts. All I want now is the money. I'll split it with you ninety-ten," Brad said.

I tried to stammer something out.

"What am I thinking?" Brad said before I could manage even a word. "I will take it all. You're the one going to jail for a helluva long time if you don't give me the money. Come on, *Cinnamon.*"

"Calm down, Brad. I don't have it," I managed, my tongue dry as sandpaper.

"Yeah. Whatever."

"I don't have it, Brad. I swear!" *Oh shit, I'm going to die. This oaf is going to kill me.*

"You may not have it, but you know where it is, so take me there. I get the money; you get to drive away. I leave Kansas, and you can go rob some other bank somewhere else. Nobody will ever know. We all win," Brad said snidely.

I needed to buy time. "I got it stashed out in the country."

"Well, let's go," Brad said, buckling his seat belt in my VW.

The only way I knew to go was to head south out of town toward my old stomping grounds. I thought maybe if we got to the old garage where I had such good luck with Ringo, I could somehow overpower or trick this psycho. Maybe I could grab a tool or something and go Rambo on this guy.

There are two different ways I could get to the farm. I could go straight through or take the "good" road. Going "straight through" is rural-person talk for taking the shortest route, but it might not be the best road. It could be bumpy or incredibly rocky. It could be sandy or terribly muddy. After a rain, you don't ever want to go straight through in Kansas. You'll probably get stuck, and even if you don't get stuck, all your neighbors will hate you for messing up the road because your car or truck will leave huge ruts.

I almost never went straight through to get out that way, but for some reason, I did this time—maybe a gun pointed at you by some pizza-making psycho impairs your decision-making ability. Like I said, I didn't pay attention well enough in the two psychology classes I took.

Right away, as I entered the road that led to our old farm, I regretted my decision to take this route. The road was dry enough and passable, but it was bumpy, and I had a guy holding a gun pointed at me who was trembling and obviously not making rational decisions. The tires on a Volkswagen Golf are not very big, and they don't absorb the ruts in an untended road very well.

Dad would sometimes call the county agent and ask about getting someone out to smooth over the roads. That was Farm Dad. He was always pleasant with others when he met or called them. Once we moved to town, Dad, Town Dad, was usually gruff and demanding when he dealt with others. I know the teachers at the school and other business folks didn't care for him much because of his jagged demeanor. I was wishing Farm Dad would have called and got someone to smooth out the ruts so I wouldn't hit a big one that might cause the gun in crazy Brad's hand to go off.

We were about a fifteen-minute drive from the garage, and there was only about thirty minutes of daylight left. I had to come up with a decision; my future, heck, my life, was depending on it. Why did Brad have to stop in for a beer at the House? Talk about your Humphrey Bogart moment. My panicked mind conjured up a vision of a poster hanging in my favorite burger joint. Humphrey Bogart in a white dinner jacket with his famous quote blazoned in gold script print: "Of all the gin joints in all the towns in the world." *Oh man, Humphrey, I totally get that line now.*

There are probably half a dozen bars within a square mile of the House of Suds. Even if twisted pizza guy had sat at a table instead of the bar, he wouldn't have heard Bo Jackson. If they played loud music in there, he wouldn't have heard her. A million variables could have steered him away from being in that very spot at that very moment.

How did he know about the cinnamon? Was that in the newspaper? Was that part of the mall gossip? Did the jerk banker tell all the managers in the mall every little detail about the robbery? I sure hope Ringo is back with his owner and happy. What a good dog. Am I going to die today?

CHAPTER THIRTY-SEVEN
FLASHBACKS

I'm pretty sure it was the first day of school, my sophomore year in high school, in our English class, when Bud Rigel asked the teacher, "If we already speak English, do we still have to take this class?" Mrs. Isaacs laughed so hard that it got us all laughing. It was the perfect icebreaker. The only other thing I remember from that class is that we read the book *In Cold Blood* by Truman Capote. It's a famous book about two psycho guys who go to a remote farm in Kansas and kill the family. They thought the farmer had a ton of cash at the house, but he didn't. It's a story of a sorrowful waste of several lives.

Anyway, we spent at least an entire week on the first page of that book! Mrs. Isaacs made us write a bunch of papers and question each other and all kinds of stuff. She was especially enthralled by one of the descriptive terms that Truman Capote used. In his description of western Kansas towns that all have those tall grain storage towers, Mr. Capote said something like *as you look across the prairie, you see a white cluster of grain elevators rising as gracefully as Greek temples, visible long before a traveler reaches them.*

She went on and on about what a beautiful and true illustration it was. The grain elevators and the comparison to the Greek temples. "How can this outsider, this writer from New York City, make such an accurate, beautiful, and poetic interpretation of what we have always seen and pretty much ignored?"

Bud Rigel said, "I think it's just cuz he writes good."

But Mrs. Isaacs would not let it rest at that. She was *way* into this Truman Capote guy, and she came up with all kinds of tasks for us about different perspectives and points of view and being a fish out of water. She could make you think and think about one simple page. Then we just read the rest of the book. Truthfully, it must have been a pretty good book because I still remember it, and it might be the only one I remember from high school.

I agree with Bud; he did write good.

CHAPTER THIRTY-EIGHT
NOSY NEIGHBORS

When Garry Grant turned in his story to his editor at the Salina Journal, he had no idea what the next day would be like for Carlos Villa. The paper guaranteed delivery by 7 a.m., and about 85 percent of the houses in town were devoted customers to the morning paper back then. A line of cars and some people on foot paraded past Mr. Villa's house from about eight in the morning, the normal time for most people to have read their morning paper, until six or seven in the evening—a normal time for people to get off work, have a bite to eat, and then read their paper.

A high-ranking official in the Salina Police Department had named Mr. Villa as a person of interest in the robbery. The robbery was pretty much the crime of the decade, and that simple declaration was enough to attract a crowd in the small town.

After about an hour of the obvious parade, Carlos came out on his front porch to look around and try to figure out what was going on.

His next-door neighbor saw him and knew he better brace Mr. Villa for what was to come.

"Hey, Carlos," the neighbor greeted Mr. Villa with a friendly tone. "How's the leg?"

"Oh, it's much better. I get to go back to work next week. Hey, what the heck is going on?"

Obviously, Mr. Villa did not get the morning paper. If he did, he would have seen his picture—the one that was on his driver's license—and a story on the front page naming him as a person of interest in the bank robbery at the mall on Black Friday.

His neighbor sheepishly handed him his copy of the paper. "Here's what this is about Carlos. I'm sure it's just a mix-up."

Mr. Villa couldn't believe his eyes.

"How could I? What is this about? Over $200,000!" Carlos looked at his neighbor. "The cops were here. They gave Ringo back to me. And now they think I robbed a bank? They never did explain to me why Ringo was in the bank. That bank got robbed?"

The neighbor excused himself as politely as he could, his head down.

Carlos wanted to say, "You don't believe this, do you?" but the neighbor had gone back inside, and when Carlos looked out, all he saw was accusing faces parading past his home.

The stream of cars and walkers, each who had easily found Mr. Villa's address in the phone book, continued all day.

CHAPTER THIRTY-NINE
VILLAIN'S MONOLOGUE

As I drove over the bumpy road, my eyes were scanning the vast expanse that is the Kansas landscape when suddenly, a clear thought hit me: *Well, ain't I Truman Freaking Capote!* I was still about three miles from the old farm place and the garage where I trained Ringo. My car was approaching an old country church and the setting sun cast a brilliant light on the church's steeple—or was it a bell tower? It was rectangular with symmetrical arches, and it rose above the Kansas vista just like Capote's graceful Greek temples.

I wondered if this might be the last time I ever gazed at the beauty of a Kansas landscape. Probably no one had ever seen it the way I was seeing it in that moment.

There was not one cell in my body that could have ever been prepared for what was happening to me. Nee Nee didn't write any papers on overwhelming anxiety and how it flips your insides around. I had never experienced this kind of turmoil. My brain felt itchy, my stomach was doing flips, and my heart and my breathing were dancing to separate fast-paced rhythms. I was amazed I hadn't soiled my underwear—yet.

A few days ago, I was shopping for shirts and ties to enter

the business world. A few days ago, I was thinking about my mom's stuffing: how it would taste and that little bit of crunch on the outer edges. I was hoping she'd use just the right amount of raisins and bake it just long enough to perfection.

Robbing a bank?

Being a hostage at gunpoint?

A life of going to class and playing an organized sport, and then selling shoes. What in the world had I ever done that could have prepared me for a moment like this? *Will these be my final moments? Are we at the end of the game, down by fifteen points, and that shot is leaving my hand? If the buzzer rings out here and my life ends, it won't matter if that shot left my hand before or after the buzzer.* I felt like I was down by fifteen points, and the clock was at five, four, three, two, one. It certainly felt like no one would hear the final buzzer.

Then, it got even more poetic. As I got closer to the church, I could see the cemetery that flanked the house of God. *Wait, what was it Nadine said? Cemetery or graveyard?* It was a graveyard because it was connected to church property. Was I driving to my grave in more than one sense?

A song came on the radio. I knew that song. Nadine liked that song. She made fun of me when I sang out the lyrics and got them all wrong. The lyrics were "Juke Box Hero," and for some reason, I thought they were singing, "Stop, drop, and roll." She was doubled over with laughter, slapping her hand on the dashboard of this very VW when she heard me sing that out loud. She had friends in Nebraska. I might have a job in Nebraska. Oh my God, I wanted to sing that song with her friends in Nebraska. I wanted her to make fun of me. I wanted all her friends to know how I messed that song up so they could all laugh and call me a goofball.

I was making a little sound I couldn't control. It was the sound a child makes when they are done crying but can't stop. It came out of me three or four times. My nose began to run, and my eyes were as misty as a November morning.

"Quit making noises like that," Brad demanded. "Unless you're going to tell me more about the robbery. No, I don't want to know. I just want the money. All two hundred thousand and some odd dollars."

I had to slow the car to make a steep left-hand turn at the bottom of a slope right as we got to the graveyard.

This might be my only chance, I thought to myself. I quietly opened the car door a small crack. I wasn't wearing a seatbelt—few of us did in 1987—and I bailed out. That's right, just like they do in the movies. It wasn't a perfect stunt-man type of leap because I caught my hip and a foot going out. I bounced off my hip and elbow without too much pain, rolled over, and started running. I spotted a utility shed on the east end of the grave-yard. Maybe I could find a rake, shovel, or something to defend myself with. I ran for all I had. I was dodging gravestones of all sizes and shapes, and I really couldn't run in a straight line due to the seemingly random pattern of gravestones. Some of the markers were three or four feet tall, while some stuck out of the grass only three or four inches. I was able to find a path, two sunken ruts, really, that led to the shed I was hoping would provide me with a solution.

Then I heard it. A gunshot. And another.

The freaking psycho was shooting at me!

I looked back over my shoulder and saw that my car had rolled into the white, corral-style fence that surrounded the graveyard. Then I saw Brad running after me. I had heard two shots so far, but there could have been others. I didn't know. I also didn't know anything about guns. The only time I'd ever been around guns was one time Coach B had us out to his place a little ways outside of town. He had a couple of shotguns, and a few guys shot some clay pigeons, skeet shooting they call it in

Kansas. He also had a couple of pistols he let us try out. That was the only thing I shot. Coach tossed a couple of old rubber basketballs twenty or thirty yards out into a muddy field, and we took shots. I fired a pistol about four or five times, but I never did hit one of the basketballs.

I was wishing I had some decent running shoes on. On the last day at the shoe store, I had worn a popular pair of loafers called Earth Shoes. They were slip-ons with a wedge on the bottom that felt like you were walking uphill. Weird and trendy. Not designed for the four-hundred-forty-yard dash.

I glanced back, and I saw Brad stumble awkwardly. As a basketball player, I knew exactly what had just happened. He rolled his ankle. If you've played much basketball, you've rolled your ankle and seen other guys roll their ankles. I bet he stepped on one of those little, short grave markers. It's like landing on another guy's foot when you come down with a rebound. It sends a shooting pain through you like some Canadian lumberjack just whacked you with a sledgehammer on the ankle. Those waves of pain shoot through your lower body and gain control of your entire being. My sixty-yard lead on him easily became a hundred-yard gap in no time. He could barely walk. I knew exactly how his ankle felt—except I had no sympathy for him whatsoever, like most players do when they see another player roll an ankle, even if it's your opponent.

At the far end of the graveyard was the wood-frame maintenance shed. Maybe it would be my safe place. Maybe it had a phone. The nearby church was deserted on a Friday afternoon. This was my only hope.

The door to the shed was slightly open, and I was shocked to see a man sitting, still and calm, at a little makeshift desk facing away from the door. "Hello," I said and saw absolutely no response. "Hello there," I said, trying to calm my breathing to appear like a normal person and not some wacko running for his life through a graveyard. I raised my hand to knock on the frame of the door.

Then I saw it. I recognized it.

This man was deaf, and he had no idea I was there. I could just tell by his posture and his non-response. I'd seen it many times with Marilyn and her friends. It's hard to explain a non-event. I asked Marilyn one time, using sign language, if she thought about hearing very often and what it would be like. She asked me if I thought about flying around like a bird very often. That explained a little of her world to me, but I always had doubts.

When I stepped through the door and gave two polite knocks, he felt the vibration in the room and turned in his chair.

I approached from the side and offered a friendly wave of my hand in his periphery.

He smiled. He started to grab something out of his shirt pocket, but before he did, I greeted him in American Sign Language.

A welcoming grin came over his face. He told me, using sign language of course, his name was George.

After a few quick pleasantries, I didn't know what to do or say to him.

I needed help.

So, I told him. My sign language wasn't that great, but he got the message. I told him that a bad and crazy man was chasing me. Where could I hide?

He told me that the church was all locked up. And it was getting dark. In a graveyard. Talk about spooky. A man was chasing me. With a gun. In a graveyard. Yeah, I know I may be a little repetitive on that point, but it was a freaking *graveyard*.

Oh, how I wanted to hear Nadine tease me about those song lyrics. I just wanted to sing that song with friends and laugh. I could even sell shoes in Nebraska. People in Nebraska need shoes too. What would be wrong with that? Would I even see next Thanksgiving and eat with my family again? Who would miss me?

Then he told me—and he had to tell me twice—that I could hide in the grave that had just been dug. He pointed to where it was: a hole next to a green carpet, sort of like AstroTurf, covering a mound of dirt.

I wanted to say that was crazy, but I thought of Brad shooting his pistol at me.

Before I darted away, I told George to be careful.

George reached into his shirt pocket and held out the card he always carried: *My name is George, and I am deaf. I love the St. Louis Cardinals baseball team and the Lord, possibly in that order.*

I ran out of the shed and looked back where Brad was. In the diminishing light, I could barely see him. He was limping badly but still headed my way. About forty yards from the shed, was the open grave. I approached it as the sun dipped behind the sandy hills in the west.

I got to the grave and could see there was a casket inside. *Dang. This guy, or gal, must have just got buried today.* I hated to do it, but I jumped in and landed with both feet on the lid of the casket. It wasn't a beautiful oak casket like my grandpa had been buried in. It was probably pine, but it did have a nice finish of varnish on it to give it a little shine. It was only a slight grade above plywood. I could barely see it with the disappearing light and the fact that it was a few feet in the ground. I stood on the casket and crouched, with my eyes just peeping above ground level, looking for Brad.

He was beginning to move a little better. That's typical for a rolled ankle. You walk it off, and if it's not broken, you can be back in the game and maybe only miss five or six minutes of playing time. I could see his ankle was coming around and he'd quickly be back up to game speed. He was picking up his pace, and just as I feared, he was heading to the shed. *God, I hope he doesn't harm George!*

As he entered the shed, I noticed a shining ceremonial shovel sticking in a mounded pile of dirt near the grave. Maybe I should just grab the shovel, hide behind the AstroTurf-covered pile of dirt, and try to smack Brad in the head with the shovel. It was dark, and I now had a plan. This plan would work. I had to make it work if I ever wanted to play basketball and volleyball in a middle school gym late at night. I wanted to play cards and drink pop by the liter, and I wanted Nee Nee to tease me about song lyrics while she sat on her boyfriend's lap in a small Nebraska farming community. She could kiss him on the face, and heck, she could marry him, and I'd go and dance on a makeshift dance floor at the wedding and drink beer with guys from Nebraska and wish them well. Oh, I had to make this work.

I saw Brad leave the shed and throw George's card to the ground with a furor in his walk. He shook his head in disgust. I'd seen that dismissive look of disgust lots of times. Mr. Bigshot at the bank acted that way toward the deaf kid who couldn't get his coffee right. You know who else had that dismissive, superior look? My dad. Every time his logic and my desires didn't match up, he'd just shake his head like I was too stupid to see things his way. *Good thing you got that expensive college education so you could know the difference between a size nine and a size ten shoe!*

I reached up out of the grave to get the shovel, but I couldn't quite reach it. Some dirt fell in the hole, and as I squatted and looked at Brad, I could tell he must have heard something. He started to move my way. *Oh shit. Shit. Shit. Shit.*

It was dark. He was within pistol range now if he was any good with that gun. He had missed me from fifty or sixty yards, but he wouldn't miss from ten or twenty.

I tried to get the lid on the casket open. It took me a few seconds to figure it out, but I got it and climbed in.

Climbed into a casket.

With a body in it.

In a grave.

At night.

My first thought was, as my elbow landed on this guy, *dang, this thing is hard*. I pulled the lid down over myself, but it didn't shut completely. I heard Brad walk by. I could tell he thought I was hiding behind the dirt pile as I heard him scampering around. Then, I think he started off in another direction. Then I heard him getting closer. He was near, very near.

My senses were correct. And my breathing was betraying me. I was breathing fast, and it was so dang quiet in that graveyard. The weirdest thoughts were flying through my brain. I wanted to play ten-point pitch again with Nadine. A sound was coming out of me. I was . . . whimpering again . . . like a scared pup might, I guess. More random thoughts were racing through my head: I wanted to talk to Mom about how her mashed potatoes are always just right. I wished I was riding in an old dusty, pollen-infested tractor cab with Dad telling me how to keep the rows running nice and straight when you planted them. I wanted to tell Mr. Cole thanks for all the Jeopardy games and for the scholarship, even though I had messed everything up. I couldn't stop breathing hard. I got the whimpering to subside a little.

I heard him stop. He kicked a little dirt onto the casket. I couldn't control my breathing.

"This is perfect," he said. "I hear you in there, shoe boy. This is better than I could have planned it. All I have to do now is tell the cops you did it. They will find the money at some point. At least I will get a reward." He was chuckling.

"And they will never find you because you're never getting out of that box. I'm going to shoot you . . ."

While he was talking, I noticed that the rock-hard item I had landed on when I jumped into the casket with the deceased was a large handgun. In fact, there were two handguns with me in the casket. This old boy must have loved guns, and his family made sure he took his loves with him. I had no idea if they would work, if they were loaded, or if the safeties were on. But when I heard Brad Phillips say, "I'm going to shoot you," I remembered Coach B's yearly speech about making the pass RIGHT NOW! Well, Coach B, your coaching might have only been 50/50, but you sure had an accurate forecast of the future. We weren't on a basketball court, but Coach's words quickly played across my mind: *And then the bad guy just stands there with a gun, and he talks on and on. . . .*

I aimed one of the guns up from my abdomen—this bugger was heavy—and pulled the trigger.

Holy cow! The noise was deafening, and the kick in the pistol was tremendous. Nothing at all like the little pistol I had fired at Coach B's house.

Almost instantly, a heavy thud hit the roof of the casket.

Then, the casket was full of smoke. In this small space, the smoke was choking me. My nose and throat were sending messages to my brain that we were not going to survive. My ears were ringing, sending out true waves of pain. There couldn't be much air left in here. Pain and panic. Two friends that you really don't want to come to your brain at the same time!

What was that thud? Did Phillips jump down onto the casket to kill me? Should I try to get the other gun? Would the first one I used fire more than once?

Had he thrown dirt on the casket? It was way too big of a thud. It was like 175 pounds landed on the cheap pine box. In fact, I could hear the screws or nails straining against the new weight.

What I didn't hear was Brad. In the movies, they say a last word, or they wriggle around a lot. I heard nothing. Such silence. Not a bird at this time of night or even an insect at this time of year . . . Unequal calm outside, while my insides were letting loose like a burst of compressed air. I feared I was running out of oxygen, so I had to open the casket. If Brad was there, I would just have to try to bargain for my life or use a pistol again.

I could barely get the lid lifted because Brad's body, his very *dead* body, was draped on top of the casket.

CHAPTER FORTY
MEANWHILE, BACK IN SALINA

M essage left on Joel Howard's message machine.

"Hey Joel, it's Nadine again. My friend I told you about, with the management job at the grain business? He's scheduling interviews . . . So, I um, kind of told him you could do an interview at 1 p.m. on Monday. So, it's Friday night about eight. I put in a good word for you. Hope you can make it. I just have a good feel about this. Tell your folks and Marilyn I said hi."

CHAPTER FORTY-ONE
DUST TO DUSK

I don't suppose many people have ever climbed out of an occupied casket and then out of the grave it rested inside. Not an easy task. I dusted myself off and went over to the shed to check on George. I was hoping the psycho pizza man hadn't hurt George. The graveyard caretaker was changing into a jacket and looked as if he was leaving for the day.

"Did he bother you?" I signed out the best I could.

George just smiled and told me he handed him his card and the bad man left. I asked George what he would say if people were looking for the bad man. George told me with his smile and his signs, "I will give them this card, and they will leave. It's how it always is."

I asked George if I could throw the dirt on the open grave.

He told me I could if I wanted to, and he would finish the job at first light. He waved and headed off. Then, he turned around and asked me how I knew sign language. I told him about Marilyn. He told me he had two sisters. Then he gave me an incredibly deep look of acceptance and trust. I hope I returned it with the same dignity. George turned and left. I never saw him again. I hope his life was rewarding.

I filled the hole to the top, and I tamped the dirt down the best I could, but there was still a lot of dirt left. I tried not to think of the man I had just put in that grave. There was one small tinge of pink left in the western sky that peeked around the dark tree trunks and empty limbs. I'm glad it was dark as I threw dirt over a body I couldn't see. And I was glad he was face down as I covered him with dirt. But he had tried to kill me. He hadn't cheated in a pickup game of basketball or a dorm room game of cards. He didn't try to trick me or hurt me or blackmail me or kidnap me. No, he tried to kill me—more than once, and I guess my mind was that of, *He was out to kill me, and I had to take care of myself or die trying.*

I made the walk across the spooky graveyard, at night, back to my car that I had ditched into the fence at the graveyard. (It had caused almost no damage to the fence; any handyman could easily fix it.) The way the silence, the darkness, and the graveyard were all present, I said out loud, "I need Truman Capote to describe this . . . Feels like a Humphrey Bogart movie."

I drove to Salina with a trunk full of cash and a ringing in my ears that would not cease. When I walked into my rented triplex, the message machine was blinking. My hands were shaking as I pushed the button to hear the recording. It was Nadine. I was heading to Nebraska. I was finally happy.

CHAPTER FORTY-TWO
A PROPER EULOGY FOR JOE MILLER

The mood at the House of Suds turned mostly somber when Debra and the two Miller boys walked in after the funeral. A quiet respect was shown by the patrons and the staff at the House. For various reasons, none of them had attended the funeral. After two or three minutes of obvious awkwardness, the younger Miller son rose up, hoisted a beer, and said, "I have an announcement."

A few shushes later and the younger Miller son spoke, at first his voice a little broken, but he picked up steam and a steady tone as he went. "I know those of you who knew our dad . . . well, he liked hanging out with every one of you. He may have been a little gruff to ya at times, especially you, Tony," he gestured toward a patron with a frosty mug, "but trust me, he was happy to be in any of y'all's presence at any time. And one more thing. You don't have to worry about our Pa. He went to church a lot as a young man, and if that ain't good enough, and he does meet the devil, don't worry about Pop, he's packing!"

And the other brother chipped in, "And they're loaded!"

An instant mood-lifter, this brought both applause and laughter from all the regulars at the House of Suds.

Debra looked at her brothers. "You lying little shits! I knew you didn't sell those Colts!" She gave her brothers that big sister look that meant, *I love you, and oh, by the way, I am also the boss of you.*

CHAPTER FORTY-THREE
SETTING THE RECORD STRAIGHT

I managed to get a few hours of sleep, packed up my stuff, and left an envelope for my roomie with $200 in it. It wasn't money from the bank. I wasn't ready to start spending *that* money yet, and I was definitely running low on personal cash until I got my last couple of checks from the shoe store.

I picked up a *Salina Journal* newspaper out of a machine on my way out of town, drove through McDonald's for a pop and a breakfast sandwich, and headed north. I tossed the paper on the front seat and saw a story about the robbery. There was a picture of a guy and a story claiming he was a person of interest. I was trying to drive and read the article at the same time but wasn't having much success, so I pulled over to read the article. And then I read it again. And again. And the whole time my mind was like, *What the hell? Where did they get this garbage?*

So, I had an hour to think as I drove to Concordia, one of the last towns in Kansas before you cross over into Nebraska. I decided I had some phone calls to make. I went into a Kwik Shop in Concordia, bought a phone card, and put $20 on it. It was only the second time I had tried one of these new phone cards, so I hoped I would be able to get it to function correctly. The operator working the information desk kindly gave me the phone number I was seeking. After a lot of number punching: card number, pin, and the phone number I was trying to call, I was able to make my first call: to Carlos Villa.

The phone rang three or four times, and someone picked up the receiver and loudly said, "Leave me alone!" and hung up.

It took me three tries—that's a *lot* of number punching—to say quickly, "I know who did it."

He waited for a second. "What did you say?"

I told him, "I know who did it, Carlos. I will tell the police and the newspaper. I will tell them today."

I could tell by his silence that he was waiting for me to tell him more. He had been put in a tough spot, and any information that could get him out of trouble was welcome. I gave him a few details about the dog that would prove to him I had exact information that would make sense to him. Information that would free him from this horrible nest of troubles he had been tossed into.

"Hey, um, Mr. Villa, I have a question. Was there any certain cop I should talk to?" I asked.

"Well, the first two officers who talked to me, they were real nice. They brought my dog back to me, and I thought that was it. They were just glad I got Ringo back safely, and then they went on their way," Mr. Villa explained.

"Were there any more cops involved?" I asked.

"One more came the next day, and he was very rude. He said he was a captain or corporal or something. I don't know nothing about ranks in the police or the army or nothing. He looked through my kitchen. He went through my cabinets, left a mess. He looked through the backyard. He said some nasty stuff about my brother and me. He was rude," Mr. Villa reiterated.

"Do you remember his name?" I asked.

"His name was Crowder or Crowley or something," Mr. Villa said with a little doubt sticking to his voice.

"As soon as I hang up with you, I will call the cops. You have nothing to worry about," I explained.

The line was silent for about five seconds, and then Carlos said, "Well, who did it then?"

"I will tell you after I tell the police and the newspaper," I assured him.

I got the number from information for the police station and the newspaper on the same call. Information, 411, would give you two numbers at a time. If you wanted more than that, they would start charging you. The phone company wasn't in business to make *you* money. I punched in the huge series of numbers, and a dispatcher at the police station answered.

"Salina PD, may I help you?"

"Hello. I'd like to speak to an Officer Crowder," I said, trying to sound calm and in charge, but the truth was, as soon as she said "Salina PD," my heart was pounding, and my belly was jumping with some kind of bowling-ball-sized butterflies. Paranoia turned on a movie in my head that featured cops sitting in a white van with listening devices that could eavesdrop on any call from Moscow to the smallest town in Kansas. These agents were sure to figure out I was the bank robber and race up in unmarked cars, blocking my way out of the phone booth.

"It's *Captain* Crowder, and what would this be in regard to?" She was pretty short with me.

"Ma'am, this is long distance, and I'd just like to speak to Captain Crowder."

I thought the long-distance ploy would work; it would work with a college kid for sure. Unfortunately, this dispatch cop didn't really care about some young guy's budgetary concerns.

"If you can tell me what the call is . . ."

I decided I'd try one more ploy. "Ma'am, I've got one minute left on this phone card, and it's about the bank robbery. The one on Black Friday."

"I'll get him if he's here," came out as the most emotionless statement you can imagine.

It's weird, but her voice at that moment made me think of that comedy about Spiccoli—no, I mean *Ferris Bueller's Day Off*. When the teacher is taking roll call, and he drones on, "Bueller . . . Bueller . . ."

About fifteen seconds later, a voice, totally large and in charge, came over the phone. "This is Captain Crowder. What is your concern?"

I decided to disguise my identity a little by playing up some kind of uneducated redneck. I had practiced it on the one-hour drive. It would not have garnered me an Academy Award, possibly a nomination for a Razzie, though.

"I seen in the *Saleena Journal* you got a person of interest in the bank robbery."

Nobody who lives in Salina pronounces it Saleena. As we always said in junior high when we would go there for a summer baseball tournament, "We're going to Salina, and that rhymes with vagina," and our mothers would say, "All right, knock it off, you hooligans."

Crowder sounded annoyed. "Yeah. I've got work to do, so get to the point."

"He's not your guy. I robbed the bank," I said.

"Oh ya did, did ya?" Crowder sounded totally bored with my revelation.

"Yep. So, take notes. I stole the dog. I trained the dog. The halter on the dog was a Pure Pet brand, halter style," I confessed.

Crowder wanted to interrupt me. "Hey—"

I wouldn't let him stop me.

"I sprinkled cinnamon into the drop slot at about midnight on Black Friday. Ringo, the dog, bit down on the bags, one or two at a time, and I hoisted him up to me. I wore a navy blue stocking hat, full mask style. I used a two-foot stepstool to be so tall the camera couldn't see my face. I tossed my coat, face mask, gloves, and a pair of black scissors I used to cut the dog's leash, and the remainder of the leash into a trash can at the Burger King, the one at the south end of town."

This is the info that grabbed Crowder by the neck—this was the truth. I could feel his icy demeanor through the phone line as soon as I said Burger King. They must have found the stuff at Burger King.

"What'd you do with the money if it was you?" he asked.

"Oh, it was me. I have the money, sorry ass. I tore the checks up into minute pieces nobody will ever find," I said.

"How did you know about these bags in the first place?" Crowder asked.

"Every bank has a night deposit; you think this is the first time I've done this?" I asked, taunting him.

I had practiced that part. I didn't lie to him. I just asked him if he thought this was my first time. He didn't answer. I could feel him starting to get pissed. I bet he was thinking about all the homework he was going to have to do to try and figure out what other banks had been robbed with this method. He'd never heard of it happening before.

"Oh, one more thing," I said. "My name is Brad. Brad Phillips. I was the manager at one of the businesses in the mall. You can do the investigation. Shouldn't take you long if you like pepperoni pizza. Oh, and you'll never find me."

"Well, Mr. Brad Phillips—"

I interrupted, "Oh dang, I lied . . . I just remembered one *more* thing. I'm going to call that reporter at the *Salina Journal* and tell him exactly what I just told you. Have a nice day," and I hung up.

I drove down the street to a different phone booth in case the cops had some kind of technology that could figure out at super-fast speed where the call came from. I was punching numbers in as fast as I could. Good thing this phone had push buttons and not the dial type—it would take forever to dial this many numbers. My heart was pounding like crazy. I called the reporter at the *Journal* whose name appeared in the byline above the story.

"*Journal*. This is Garry Grant," his voice sounded confident—and important.

I gave him the straight dope as fast as I could. I expressed that I wanted to see Crowder catch a little heat for his shoddy treatment of Mr. Villa.

"I can't guarantee that will happen. We hafta keep a good relationship with the police, or they won't talk to us," Garry explained.

"Well, if they *are* feeding you BS, I don't know why you would want to keep talking to them. I gotta go, sir. I am sharing this same information with Mr. Villa. Hopefully, he can regain a peaceful life. I would think *you* would want to apologize to him." And before he could respond, I hung up.

CHAPTER FORTY-FOUR
JULY 2024

I still remember that drive. That wonderful, freedom-seeking drive out of Kansas. It was about a thirty-mile trek from that phone booth to the Nebraska state line. When you entered the state, there was a huge green billboard that welcomed you with the slogan "Nebraska, The Good Life."

I was certainly hoping that would be an accurate description of what lie ahead.

Nebraska.

Got the job. Got the friends.

The friends. Oh, man, did we have fun. We played cards and a crazy group dice game called Bunko. We played basketball, volleyball, badminton—anything to get together and have fun. Most of our play group were teachers. We had the run of the school after hours. A gymnasium to use on nights and weekends. A Home Ec room if you needed a sewing machine. A woodshop if you needed to borrow some tools. The school was like an extension of our homes. Of course, as we got a little older, people got married and had kids. This turned our play group into more of a barbecue group, but we still stayed connected for the most part. We supported each other as friends in a small town do.

Oh, and one last little piece of luck. The first or second time we played some basketball at the gym, I sat down on the first row of the bleachers to change out of my work shoes into my basketball shoes. I was wearing those same Earth Shoes I had worn the day I . . . uh, *jumped into a casket with a dead guy.* After thirty-plus years, that is still a pretty weird sentence to ponder.

Anyway, I take off my shoe and the guy I'm sitting near is like, "Woah, classic Earth Shoes. I have a pair of those. I think I've only worn them one time! They are so weird."

"Yeah, I worked at a shoe store, so I've got every kind of loafer made in the last three years," I said.

He picked up my shoe to examine its weird structure and then said, "What the actual hell?"

"What?" I asked.

He held up the shoe, turned what little heel there was on it toward me, and I could see a perfect brass circle in the bottom of the heel.

"Dude, that is a bullet. Someone shot your shoe!" he was flabbergasted.

My mind was working on two fronts. One: *Do I have to come up with a phony story?* I could say that one day, I was at a buddy's house, and we had a contest to see who could shoot the shoe from the farthest distance.

Mind-front number two: *That crazy pizza guy, Brad Phillips, missed shooting me in the heel by about one inch—or less! If that bullet had hit my foot, well, I wouldn't be sitting where I am today, that's for sure.*

Before I could offer a possible explanation, he concocted his own story, which was fine with me. He figured some crazed warehouse worker thought it would be fun to shoot a box of shoes one day on his break, and that's just where the slug landed. I was plenty happy to nod in agreement and say, "Well, those warehouse jobs probably get a little tedious at times."

I'd go years without thinking about that day in the graveyard and Brad Phillips. Then, something in my mind would break the seal, and the memories would shoot through me like a burst of compressed air in a stopped city bus.

My brain was pretty good at blocking out the Brad Phillips chapter of my life. Sometimes, an uncontrollable wave of guilt or terror would arise, almost like a turbulent blush, intent on sending me spiraling out of normalcy. But my mind would circle back to the fact that Brad Phillips wasn't just an unfortunate raccoon on US 385 in western Nebraska. He wasn't the unlucky linebacker slipping on a puddle in a dormitory laundry room. Brad Phillips had chased me through a graveyard and fired shots at me with the intent to kill. If Brad had had his way, I would have never met my wife and never had two great daughters who have both married lucky and given us three amazing grandkids. Maybe it's not fair the human brain works this way, but I'm glad the luck was on my side and Brad Phillips wound up like he did.

I guess I can freely tell you the rest of the story. Nadine was with the same guy for years, like ten or twelve, but they never married. Then, one summer, she did a teaching seminar on the East Coast, met a guy in June, and married that guy on Labor Day. Beautiful wedding about two blocks from Fenway Park. My wife and I went to Boston and truly enjoyed the ceremony and the celebration, even though Nadine's mom did throw an occasional zinger at her daughter. Everyone just laughed and chalked it up to the alcohol, even though Mrs. Blass never touched a drop of the stuff. Nee Nee joined her husband out east, and they live in Connecticut, where she still teaches middle school. "For one or two more years," she tells me.

My wife was a friend of Nadine's. She taught business classes at the high school in Hastings for her entire career. Mom taught her how to make the stuffing and the mashed potatoes to perfection! We had two kids, three dogs, and a few cats over the years. I never did give my wife a nickname. I called her by her given name our entire marriage.

Before we got married, my wife insisted I patch stuff up with my dad.

"If you can't fix your relationship with your dad, what makes you think you could fix things between us when we have rough spots?" That was the accounting teacher in her, I guess. The ledger had to balance. The debits and the credits had to be reconciled.

It was maybe the best thing that happened. I started having really good talks with Dad, and for the last ten years of his life, for the most part, we enjoyed each other's presence. One time, we were up here in Nebraska fishing at a beautiful private pond, and I caught a nice walleye. Well, as I was removing the hook, the little bugger got away, and I made a desperate scoop with a small handheld net. In a stroke of good fortune, I pulled him right out of the water and dropped him in a bucket.

"You always have been a lucky duck," Dad said. Pretty typical assessment from him—short and to the point with a crusty cliche to show his age. His relational tool kit was missing a few things, but I certainly had my issues too.

The money? I used some to get me settled in Nebraska, but I kept close track of it so I could fulfill my purpose.

I gave a little over $120,000 to three different schools that serve hearing-impaired students in Nebraska and Kansas. I used an alias; I was Bill Jones most of the time, or Jen Johnson, and a few times, I was Morty Givens. I thought a guy named Morty Givens would be a generous son of a gun, so he sent quite a bit of money their way. Pre 9/11, it was easy to set up a fake bank account and give money away. Those days are gone. I gave most of the rest to area schools here in Hastings, the majority going to study programs for at-risk kids and junior league basketball. I easily cleared the $138,038 because, after several years of just simply giving, I finally figured out how to seed money properly. Multipliers abound when you have money.

For instance, one of my daughters loved volleyball. So, we

hosted a volleyball tournament and designated a charity to be the recipient of the funds raised. Because we had a good pot of money to start with, we could put on first-class events of all types: sports, concerts, wine tastings, square dancing, and horse and dog shows to support childhood cancer or after-school programs. People who came to our events were sometimes incredibly generous, and their giving would astound us when we totaled up the funds. You name it, we kept busy, and the money we raised went to charities all over Nebraska.

So, the number is way over $250,000. I quit tracking it after I had crossed the $138,038 mark. My career was financially rewarding and my investments over time have done well. When I check out of this life, my Trust will drop a pretty good buck into several good causes, most of them related to assisting deaf children and adults.

Remember when I told you that if I were to start this story at the end, I'd be leaving my lawyer's office? Well, I told him all about the bank robbery, and he just sort of grinned and clapped his hands together. "Way past statute of limitations on the money. Nothing anybody can do about it."

He had one of those goofy triangle golf tee puzzles on his desk, exactly like the one Skinny Sanderson had back at the insurance agency thirty-plus years ago. "Your Trust is all in order. Go, enjoy your life."

End of the story? Hmmm. Life can have some funny turns and twists. And funny isn't always the "ha, ha" variety. The kids are grown and flown. My wife is in hospice, nearly gone—frickin' cancer—and who knows what tomorrow may bring?

So, am I the luckiest guy in, what was it, the Northern Hemisphere? I think I rank up there pretty high.

Oh, the hospice stories. On day two of my wife being admitted to hospice, my adult daughters told me, "Go out and watch a movie or go bowling or something. You've been just sitting here for two days looking all bedraggled."

My wife would wake up and talk to us for a couple of hours at a time and then drift off to sleep. It really was a comfort to have the girls at my side.

"Just go," they demanded.

It did sound good to me to get out of there and maybe find a sports bar and watch a game with a cold bottle of beer in hand.

When I returned about two hours later, my wife was breathing just a little shallower, in a deep sleep, and my daughters looked like they had just attended a Las Vegas quality comedy show. It was a mixed-up scene to comprehend.

"Oh, Mom has been on a roll!" my eldest said, wiping tears of laughter from her eyes.

"She should have been a Hollywood scriptwriter. These drugs they have at this place have got to be the best in the world," the younger one said.

"What? What do you mean?" is all I could manage to say. Still a little discombobulated with the sight of my daughters laughing while their mother lay in a hospice bed in the very same room.

"Wait till you hear this one Mom cooked up, Dad. You better sit down. And don't take a sip of pop unless you want it going out your nose!"

Once they gained control over the laughing fits—some of it bordered on cackling—they pieced the story together for me, each taking turns with various parts and jabbing each other on the shoulder or slapping the other one on the thigh.

My wife had told them, "Hey girls, I bet you didn't know this, but I had an affair once. I did it to keep your dad from going to prison. He robbed a bank in Kansas, and a cop from there came up to dig around and ask questions. The cop told me he had the proof, but he could maybe make that proof go away if things went a certain way. Wink, wink. Well, three or four of those Smirnoff Ice drinks—we even had beer in the fridge, don't ya know—but he wanted those Smirnoffs. Drank 'em right down. And so, I just had sex with him, and that was that. I knew he had robbed the bank cuz Nadine told me. You girls were like in middle school at the time, so I figured I better do something to keep your father out of jail."

They interrupted their own story. "Can you believe this? Ms. Blass! The science teacher! Remember her? I'm telling you, the drugs in this place are way better than anything the cartels have for sale."

I'm trying to laugh and enjoy this, um, story, but some real-time stuff is going on inside my head.

1. How in the heck did Nadine—Nee Nee—know I robbed the bank? She was living in Nebraska at the time.
2. What the heck? Sex with a cop? Who was this cop that had—I can't even say it.
3. Maybe she just made the whole thing up. But it's too specific, especially that part about a bank in Kansas. She knew? Nadine told her? She had . . . with some cop? I can't even think it.

Of course, I decided to say to the girls, "I bet the nurses that work here have heard some of the most outlandish tales through the years." I thought that was better than saying, *Hmm, I didn't know about the sex with a cop part, and I didn't know about Ms. Blass telling your mother that I robbed a bank, but that part about me robbing a bank in Kansas a long time ago—well that was spot on girls!*

I tried to laugh it up a little and say, "Do you think we would have had that old green minivan so long if I had robbed a bank?"

CHAPTER FORTY-FIVE
BLAST FROM THE PAST

The next day, I decided I'd stop off at the grocery store and pick up one of those big plastic trays that had all kinds of cheeses, cold cuts, and veggies as I headed back to the WestEnd Hospice facility where my daughters were with my wife as she was living out her final days. Just as I was walking into the store, my cell phone rang, and it was my oldest daughter. My mind immediately went to a dark spot. *I bet she's gone.*

"Hey, Dad. How's it going?"

"I'm fine. How's your mother? Did she . . ."

"Actually, she is doing pretty well right now. The nurse said she's having a 'burst,' and it probably won't be much longer. No more crazy talk. She's just listening and smiling with her eyebrows. A day or two. But the reason I called is because you have a visitor."

"*I* have a visitor?"

"Yeah, this guy says you go way back to your days in Salina, Kansas."

"Hmmm." My curiosity was kicking in pretty good. *Probably a guy I played ball with in college just passing through Nebraska.*

"Yeah, Dad. He says his name is Brad Phillips Jr. He is just waiting with us here at the hospice. He said it will be good to see you. See you soon, Dad."

CHAPTER FORTY-SIX
DECEMBER 1987

"That car with Oklahoma plates is still out there, I see."

"It won't be for much longer, tow truck is on its way," Robert Clemons, the owner of the House of Suds, said as he bent down and placed about ten clean beer mugs in the cooler beneath the arched bar.

"Did Molly get squared away in her new place?" the bar patron asked with a gentle edge to his question.

"She did. We've tried to move her to a facility before, but the other day, after her latest public outburst, her mother was pretty determined to find a place. Some new outfit in Wichita says they are having success with that, *multiple people stuff*, or whatever it is she has."

"Did she have to get stitches?" the patron asked, not unkindly.

"Yep, five or six, right on her cheekbone. Man, I've never seen her rip out her own hair like that. I seen her do it to her little sister and her mother's hair once. God, that was an awful night." Robert shook his head.

"Well, maybe this new place will help her out."

"I hope so," Robert said. "Here, take this basket of remotes and get some games on. I gotta get some chicken breasts prepped up. Donny Wright is doing his annual company Christmas party in here, and they'll be rolling in here about noon."

CHAPTER FORTY-SEVEN
SINGLE MOM

David O'Hara was staying late at the Kinney Shoes in the Salina, Kansas, mall. It was Sunday, January 3, 1988, and David was hurriedly packing the Christmas decorations into boxes that he would unpack and then place those same decorations in the exact same spot when November rolled around. As David came from the back room to tote the last box to the storeroom, he saw a woman standing at the metal gate that was already closed for the night. They'd been closed for over thirty minutes. Someone might need emergency job interview shoes; it was a common occurrence. David didn't mind helping a person in dire need.

"Well, look who's here!" he called cheerfully.

"Hello, David."

"Looks like you have a little visitor for me to meet," David said as he approached the woman holding an infant's car seat in one hand and a diaper bag in the other.

"I sure do," Joy said.

David pushed a button that caused the chain to screech a little, and then the gate began to rise.

"This is Bradley. He's a handful for sure," Joy said.

"What a cute little guy. Oh, Joy, we sure missed you the whole Christmas season."

"There were days I would have rather been here helping out in the store, but for the most part, I've really enjoyed being home with Bradley."

"Well, not to press, Joy, but, um . . . a couple of things," David said tentatively.

"Go ahead, David. That's why I came down to talk to you." Joy smiled serenely.

"Well, one, I hate to bug ya, but are you wanting to come back to the store, and if so, when? We could *really* use you."

"No, David. I won't be coming back here. I'm going to go back to school. I want to finish my degree and then get something, well, you know . . ."

"Absolutely, Joy. I get it. If I can be of any help along the way, you let me know. I will give you a good reference. What type of career are you lookin' at?" David asked.

"Well, right after high school, I did one semester of college to be a nurse. Then, crazy me, I got pregnant and did five years with a drugged-out husband, but I got my daughter Katy, so it was worth it. Now, here I am, still a single mom for the second time, but Katy's grandpa is helping out, and we are going to move to Wichita. I'm enrolled to start classes next week. I want to get my degree in counseling."

"You'll make a great counselor, Joy. But first, we gotta have a going away party for you. I'll spread the word among the mall employees. Everybody's going to want to wish you well," David insisted.

"You don't have to do that," Joy said.

"I don't *have* to, but I'm *going* to. Invite your friends. I'll take care of the rest. White cake or chocolate?" David asked.

"Either is fine. It does sound fun. Hey, invite Joel. I haven't seen him in a while," Joy said.

"Okay. Sheesh, I haven't seen Joel since his last day here. He was supposed to work down at Skinny's insurance office, and then, poof! He just disappeared. Oh, Joy, you're going to do so well in college and beyond."

"Well, I hope so. Hey, David. I, um . . . is Brad around? Like, still working at the pizza place?" Joy asked nervously.

"Have not seen him since the week after Thanksgiving. Just like Joel: Poof. Gone. It's weird, they both just sort of vanished . . . at the same time. Sheesh. There was a whole bunch of activity around the pizza place. Cops. Newspaper and radio guys. The word going around was that the regional manager came in and fired Brad. Right after the bank heist! The rumors were he messed up some bank deposits or something. Nobody's seen him since." David shook his head.

"We talked two or three nights before he disappeared. He said his goal was to get his own store down in Oklahoma. He said he'd support the baby—*if*, get this, I named the baby Bradley.

I hate to admit this, but the only thing on my mind was being able to pay rent and buy diapers. So, I was like, sure, Bradley is a fine name. He also said we could be a couple, but I ruled that out. We were *never* going to be a couple. One stupid night of drinking. I feel like such a fool, David. If he ever shows his face in this mall again, will you please give him my new address and phone?"

David took the card Joy handed him and carefully placed it in his wallet. He was truly concerned that Joy was in for a tough go as a single mom trying to make it on her own, but he knew that her gentle, caring spirit could take her far in the world of college and service to humanity.

CHAPTER FORTY-EIGHT
JULY 2024

J oy Costa was enjoying her free weekend. She aimed her Jeep Cherokee down Highway 400 through eastern Kansas on her way to the Lake of the Ozarks in southern Missouri. Her sister owned a nice lakeside cabin that Joy would be enjoying for the next three days with her son Bradley, his wife, and their three kids. Tubing, fishing, swimming, and board games would fill their weekend. The five-hour drive would all be worth it once Joy was watching her grandkids play at the lake before the sun went down.

A drive like this was always a time of quiet reflection and a battle to push work worries to the side. The Oasis Counseling Center would still be there waiting for her when she returned on Tuesday. This was a time for peace, quiet, and family.

After only thirty miles, Joy's quiet mindset was losing out to her check-list mindset, so she decided to turn on one of her favorite podcasts. *Melody's Musings* was a podcast Joy had stumbled upon when talking to another therapist. She had given it a try and liked Melody's style, whether she was interviewing guests or just talking. Melody always had a soothing, positive message that Joy likened to having your grandma around when you were a little kid. Grandma could always find the right tone of voice to put you in a listening, accepting state of being. Mom could tell you the exact same thing, but coming from Grandma, it just resonated with perfection.

Melody was interviewing a guest while Joy's Jeep Cherokee, packed with pool toys and snacks for the grandkids, motored its way east down Highway 400.

"Today I am thrilled to have in my very own studio a guest who has some stories to share. His name, well let's call him Bill, and let's say he is from, how about Florida, Bill? Does Florida sound like a good, fictional spot for you?"

"That sounds great," this Bill said. "I can be Bill from Florida today."

"Okay, Bill from Florida, first tell the folks a little bit about your life and background, and then we will get to the part where you and I became work partners. I like to think of you as a partner in my work because, as I always say on this show, I cannot perform any type of therapy services without a willing, working partner."

Bill went on to explain how he bounced around in a few odd jobs as a young man and then decided to give law enforcement a try. He started as a county deputy in a very small department and then transferred to a nearby city. He then worked his way up in the police force, all the way to the top, and retired as a captain.

Melody then talked about post-traumatic stress disorder and said it was one of the fastest-growing conditions that therapists were seeing. She said this growth in awareness needed to come about for years, but the emphasis on mental health being a true element of general human health seemed to be a catalyst for the number of clients suffering from PTSD. She had a soothing way of talking about difficult topics and that was probably why her podcast was gaining listeners by the thousands.

Bill answered her questions the best he could about his

career, and the interview sort of became a confessional of this cop feeling bad about some of the people he had goaded into a foot-chase so he could "run 'em down, pound 'em, and haul 'em to the jug."

Melody wanted to wrap it up on a feel-good note for her audience and asked Bill, "What was the craziest or quirkiest case you ever worked, Captain?"

"Oh, gosh, that would be a hard question. You come across some pretty crazy situations out there. Well, I tell ya, there was one I never could get outta my mind. This guy robbed a bank, one of those branches in a mall. Well, this guy stole all the night deposit bags outta this bank—on Black Friday!"

Joy's eyes went from staring out at white dotted lines disappearing beneath her Jeep to her eyes being directly fixed on her car radio where the podcast continued.

"The way he did it, he trained this tiny dog to bite down on the deposit bags, then he shoved that dog through the night slot —you know that night deposit thing that banks have? Well, he put that dog on a leash, shoved him in there, the dog grabbed the bags, he pulled the dog up, and *voila!* He got away with about two hundred thousand bucks. Oh, I can't leave this part out. He sprinkled cinnamon all over those bags. That dog must have loved cinnamon."

"JEEZO BEEZO!" Joy Costa screamed at her windshield. When he said "cinnamon," Joy nearly drove off the road, as her brain was dealing with extreme overload.

In the background, Joy could hear the podcast cop talk about how, initially, they thought it was an inside job at the bank, and the dog was just to throw 'em off. Then they thought it was a guy in town who was good at training dogs, and then on and on he droned about his theories, but they never did figure it out.

Joy Costa had figured it out, though. She knew exactly who did it, and now she knew how. She pushed the Off button on her car sound system and said right out loud, "Holy cow. I gotta call Bradley."

A string of a thousand thoughts sped through Joy's brain as she waited for her son to pick up the phone. Joy remembered the patient well. She was an attractive, spirited lady in her late forties. She was one of Joy's favorite yet most heartbreaking clients she served in her career of over twenty-five years of counseling. Molly suffered from what they called multiple personality disorder when Joy first started seeing her. Years later, and after a little progress with Molly, her malady was known as dissociative identity disorder (DID). Either way, Molly was living the life of five or six people. The one that Joy could vividly recall as the phone rang in her ear was Justine. Justine was one of the "alters" or alternative personalities that lived within her. Molly's "core" personality was a quiet daughter of a bar owner in Hutchinson, Kansas. Molly enjoyed playing darts and billiards. She was loved by her customers and could get the back room of a greasy bar and grill sparkling like it was a million-dollar NASA project.

Justine was a very difficult alter whom Joy did her best to help. Justine claimed she was a dental hygienist, which was not true. Justine also claimed to have had sexual relations with hundreds of men, which probably was true. These behaviors led Justine to find herself in dangerous situations, and in the four or five years Joy had been one of her therapists, Justine had made several trips to urgent care facilities and, on two occasions, had long stays at hospitals due to severe beatings. Joy knew the sad facts about DID. It's very rare; less than one percent of the population is affected, and it mostly occurs in women. Most of these unfortunate women had some type of sexual abuse in their background. Justine was a baby in a Romanian orphanage. Joy recalled how sad all her colleagues were the day they learned Molly was found dead from a drug overdose in a women's shelter in Tulsa.

Oftentimes, Joy would cut her sessions with Justine short because it was so heartbreaking to listen to Justine recount her liaisons with strange men. One of those encounters, however, popped into Joy's mind with the clarity of a first-rate showing at an IMAX theater. Joy remembered exactly where she was sitting. She could visualize Justine wearing the burgundy-colored scrubs she liked to wear when the dental hygienist alter took over.

"He was rich. I should have stayed with him. He had bags and bags of money in this big army duffle bag. He worked at the mall at a shoe store. I saw his nametag lying on the dresser in the hotel. He only had one weird kink. He sprinkled cinnamon on his hands and pants." Justine giggled when she thought about the cinnamon.

"I called him Cinnamon, but his name was Joel. That was on his name tag from a shoe store."

"What makes you think he had bags and bags of money?" Joy asked her client.

"Cuz, I saw 'em. I usually go through guys' stuff once they fall asleep. It's just interesting to see their stuff. But I never take anything." She then became agitated because she felt like Joy and all the other therapists never believed her claims.

"You don't believe me, do you? I have never stolen anything!" Justine dug her fingernails into the upholstery of her chair.

Joy's son Bradley picked up his phone on the third ring.

"You sittin' down, baby?" Joy asked.

"Well, no, actually. I'm unloading the kids' stuff out of the truck. We just rolled up to the cabin. What's your ETA?" Bradley asked.

"I don't know, a couple of hours or so. Sitting down or not, I just learned some stuff about your dad," Joy said.

"Really? Well, okay. I mean, did you talk to him?" Brad Jr. asked.

"No, not yet, but this whole thing is about to get real interesting."

Joy had been looking forward to a relaxing weekend at a cabin by the lake. No phones. No internet. Just the sounds of laughter of grandchildren and the smells of food on the grill. How does one act when they've solved a bank robbery that took place thirty-some years ago?

CHAPTER FORTY-NINE
UM, HELLO?

Well, I am just good and screwed.

Bradley Phillips *Junior*? Brad had a *kid*? He told me he was a single guy. The only way this guy is talking to me means that he figured this out somehow and then tracked me down. Or is this just some weird imposter? Maybe it's a cop? Maybe it's a private eye type of guy; he figured it out, and now he's going to blackmail the shizz out of me.

There are a hundred possibilities, and not one of them is favorable for me. Good gosh, my daughters are there, *with* Brad Phillips Jr. or *somebody* who is there to do me harm. Hopefully, my wife will fade away before she has to hear any of this. Somehow, I've got to get this Brad guy away from my family. I've got plenty of money, but how will it ever be enough?

That drive after the phone call was about three miles, but it felt like three hundred miles. I walked into the hospice center, and thankfully, I had a plastic container of fruit and snacks in my hands. I needed something to steady my hands because I was as nervous as an accused criminal watching their jury walk in to reveal the verdict.

I saw my two daughters standing there with a young man, a little older than my girls, probably mid-thirties. When he turned and faced me, one mystery was solved: this was no imposter. He was, without a doubt, the biological son of Brad Phillips. The DNA was undeniable. He had the same cheekbones that rode high with a reddish coloring all the way back to his ears. My life of comfort was about to take a huge dent.

He was the first one to speak. "Hi, Mr. Howard."

"Hi . . ." I tried to use body language to direct the young man to another area of the health facility. "Hey girls, let me talk to Brad over here." I handed my girls the snack tray and gave them each a weak hug.

"Sheesh, Dad," my youngest said. "You're shaking like a leaf. The nurse just told us it will be another day or two. Go ahead and talk to your friend. We'll be in Mom's room." She gave her sister a look that said, *Poor Dad, he's losing it.*

I was shaking like a leaf all right, and I *was* losing it. Sad to admit, but the losing it and the shaking were not because of my suffering wife at that very moment.

We walked across the foyer and gravitated to a table in a nook near a window. The designer of the space obviously fashioned this spot for families and medical people to have serious talks about, well, death. I was hoping the conversation I was about to have would *not* lead to my death, or any death.

I didn't know what to say, and the only thing that came to me was to ask, "Well, why are you here?"

"My mom sent me. Encouraged me anyway. It was my decision," Brad Jr. said proudly.

"And, do I know your mom?" I was stalling, I guess, hoping a tornado siren would go off and I'd be able to say, *Oh, well, storms coming. See you in ten years. Thanks for stopping by.*

"You know my mom. You worked with her for a short time in Salina, Kansas. At a shoe store. Her name is Joy Costa," Brad Jr. said.

No sirens. No earthquakes—well at least not the kind that was going to get me out of this.

"Joy at the shoe store . . ." I looked up at the ceiling and took a deep breath. "I do remember her. I didn't work at the shoe store very long, just a few months after college. Well, when were you born?"

"I figured you'd ask that." He pulled his driver's license from his shirt pocket. His name was Bradley Costa, and he was born on November 30, 1987, just one day after I robbed the bank. Good Lord, the photo on his driver's license looked exactly like his dad. All he was missing was a Sbarro name tag that read, "Manager: Brad."

"Says your name is Bradley *Costa*," I queried.

"Mom named me after my dad, first name only. I kept her last name. I never met him. I'm here hoping you can tell me why I never met him. My mom has come up with her set of facts. I want to hear *your* set of facts."

I stared straight ahead, my mind wondering how many details I should disclose and how many details I could leave out. There are lots of things he couldn't *know*, he was just fishing.

"Mom said maybe I should call you Cinnamon. She said that was a nickname you liked."

At that point I wished I could hand him a card like George always had with him: *My name's Joel, and I'm deaf.* And he'd leave me alone. That wasn't going to happen.

CHAPTER FIFTY
COLD CASE

Two hours later, we concluded what had to be the strangest meeting of my life. Two days later, I was back in my lawyer's office, and that's why I told you upfront that this story ends in my lawyer's office.

The strangest meeting of my life was at a Starbucks, not far from the WestEnd Hospice Center. Bradley followed me over there in his truck. When we arrived, I saw Joy from the shoe store get out of her Jeep and walk to Bradley. Thirty-some years hadn't really changed her that much. She still had that pep in her step that I remembered. They both looked me straight in the face. I looked down at the sidewalk like it was a tightrope and I had to concentrate to put one foot in front of the next. Darn Starbucks door was unlocked. We went in and sat down. The sky was blue, and there would be no tornado to save me from this inquisition I seemed to be facing. As I was walking in the door, all I could think was, *How do you tell someone, "I shot and buried your dad. Can I get you two a latte? I hear the espresso here gets great reviews also."*

"I don't think I would have recognized you if I had just seen you at Walmart," Joy said after a brief moment of silence.

"Well, I didn't have a gray beard at twenty-two." I tried to temper the moment with some type of grace or at least neutrality.

The niceties and the small talk lasted only about thirteen seconds.

"Just tell us everything," Bradley said.

As I took a deep breath in, holding on to the edge of the table to keep my hands from shaking, I noticed that Joy's hands and the look in her eyes were as steady as a Mennonite-built kitchen table.

"We know about the bank, the cinnamon, the dog, the money, the girl at the hotel, and the bags and bags of money. We don't care about that. We want to know about his father." Her head tilted toward Bradley. "We know Brad Phillips' 1984 Bronco II got towed from that little bar in Hutchinson about ten days after the robbery. And we know a few other things. Do you know what happened to Brad?"

This gal knew how to conduct an interview. *We know a few other things.* My mind was like a Vegas gambler determining odds. *If I tell some of the truth and lie just a little, and they catch me in that lie, then they will have zero trust and could easily destroy me. But wait, it was self-defense. He was chasing me with a gun and firing the gun! At me! I should have saved that damn shoe.* My lawyer had assured me I was totally clean on the bank stuff. My problem was the cops would probably come up with some law saying you can't bury a guy you shot and not report it. I'm pretty sure that is against some type of body-disposal law of some sort.

"I will tell you everything I know. Everything that happened. And then," my words just stopped. I was trying to think of a way to frame this when I knew that only the truth would—well, it sure didn't seem like the truth would—set me free.

"That's exactly why we're here," Joy said as Bradley leaned forward, eyeing me like a juror examining a key witness.

In three minutes, I had told them everything I could remember from the time Brad Phillips walked into that bar on that particular afternoon in Hutchinson, Kansas. I told them about the phone call he got firing him, and Bradley nodded his head as if to say, *We knew about that.*

Dang, I thought, *these two should go into cold case crime solving.* They were good. I told them about the gun, the chase through the graveyard, and Brad's death. I also told them what I did with the money—some of it anyway—I could tell they were not interested in those details.

"I'm sorry this happened to your father, Bradley. I do want to say on my behalf that I acted in pure self-defense."

"You may have," he said, as steady as his mother. "But I'm pretty sure there are laws against killing and then burying someone without going to the authorities."

My mind said, *Yeah, I kind of figured you'd say that.* I definitely didn't have a response, but he didn't make me wriggle on the hook for long.

"What good does it do me for you to get arrested and sit through some big-ass trial. Bank robber slash killer finally gets caught? The media would love it. The Kansas dog whisperer slash graveyard killer," Bradley said.

Was I being blackmailed? It was sort of feeling that way. My lawyer wasn't going to believe this. *You're in the clear, Joel. Go live your life.* He was talking about the bank and the money. *Oh, yeah, one other thing, Mr. Lawyer, sir. I sort of left out the part about the killing and the burying. I'm sure that will be okay, right?* My daughters and sons-in-law would be so ashamed of me. Good Lord, I have grandkids. I was hoping my wife would die instantly so she wouldn't have to find out about this in her final days. Maybe I could just die instantly. God, I wish I could trade places with her.

"Okay, let's back up a little first," Bradley offered. "He's not my father. He's my biological dad. That's how I think of him. That's how I've always thought of him since I was twelve years old, and Mom told me about him and the reason I have his first name. He was supposed to support Mom through my childhood. Well, he can't do that while lying in some country cemetery in Kansas."

I didn't interrupt him, but *it's a graveyard,* my brain silently messaged me.

"I guess the thing I want you to know is Mom and I have talked about this a lot ever since I had kids of my own. I'm okay. I don't need that biological dad. I had the best mom in the world —a freaking fantastic mom." Bradley straightened up and smiled at his mother.

I glanced at Joy, and I could see the pride in her eyes. I knew that pride. When my daughters graduated, got married, all that big stuff, sure, but even more in those unscripted moments when I'd see them with their kids or they hosted my wife and me for a family birthday party. It's a feeling of love that just tickles your heart. Joy had done a marvelous job raising this young man. The reddish coloring on his cheekbones had come from his father's DNA, but that steady inner strength had come from being raised by, to use his words, a freaking fantastic mom.

"And as I said before, nobody benefits from us dragging this into a media circus court case. Oh, I guess the TV stations or some true crime show could make a pretty good buck off this story, but they would just be on to the next weird crime the next day. By next Tuesday, we'd be old news, and you'd be up to your neck in lawyers' bills or wearing an orange jumpsuit. So, Mom and I have thought about this, and even though you said you did a lot of good with the money, we want you to help someone else," Bradley said.

"Okay, sure," I gladly blurted out before the Vegas odds-maker in me could even say, *Wait a minute, how much we talkin'? This could go on forever.*

"In her counseling business, my mom has worked with a lot of women over the years that are—"

"They have *various* challenges," Joy pitched in.

"Anyway," Brad continued, "Mom started up a foundation to give assistance to some of the people. She is a great counselor and life coach."

"But I'm a terrible fund-raiser," Joy admitted.

"So, you mentioned the figure of a hundred and some thousand, even though the old papers said it was two hundred thousand," Bradley said.

I was just going to hold my tongue and see where this went.

"Right now, Mom's foundation has $83 in their checking account. Well, their only account. You can't help many folks with $83," Bradley reasoned.

"The clients are vetted, and the money goes to those that can succeed if they just get a little bump. We take some bills off their table and let them get a little . . . traction."

"People need traction. All people," I said. "Most of us get it from our parents or our schooling. I got a lot of mine at the breakfast table. I had a really good mom, like you do, Bradley."

"We don't want to come off like hijackers asking for a ransom," Bradley said.

My stupid brain was like, *Kidnappers want a ransom, Bradley. Hijackers want their demands met.* Luckily, I said nothing.

"We feel like maybe ten thousand dollars would go a long way toward helping many, many clients, and you sort of . . ." his voice ran out of steam.

When he said ten thousand dollars, I figured I wasn't hearing him right. Maybe he meant to say ten thousand dollars a month or some such demand.

"Joy, Bradley, I am happy to help your foundation. I will need to visit my financial guy. And, I will have to see my lawyer. He's got all my stuff tied up in a Trust, like a Will, ya know," I explained.

I was going to have to come up with some BS story of how I learned about a new foundation that touched my heart. It was just paperwork for him; he'd bill me for it, so what the hey.

"Let's make it a hundred and thirty-eight," I said.

Joy and Bradley just kind of stared at me. I saw Bradley's throat tighten up, and his eyes narrowed in on me. "A hundred and thirty-eight dollars?"

"I can do one thirty-eight. One hundred thirty-eight thousand and thirty-eight dollars. It will take me a couple of days to move some money," I said.

"Oh! My goodness, Joel," Joy's eyes were instantly filled with tears.

CHAPTER FIFTY-ONE
LUCKY

And so, six days later, I left my lawyer's office. He still had that goofy little triangle puzzle with the golf tees sticking out. It was my last business stop of the day after paying the mortuary and leaving a thank-you card and some snacks at WestEnd Hospice Center. As I drove home, my thoughts raced right on over to where they had been taking me for the last thirty-plus years. *I am a lucky duck.* Lucky to have worked in a shoe store with a wonderful woman who raised an amazing young man who wanted to help others. Lucky that Coach B taught me not to wait around while the bad guy makes a speech about how he's going to kill you. Mostly, I'm lucky for a mom who read those newspaper articles to me every morning. I tried to be that dad, but my kids were always in a hurry or disinterested. I guess I just didn't have the knack Mom had for reading to kids over a bowl of sugared-up Rice Krispies. Not everything comes down to luck; some things require skill. Mom had the skill—and I got the luck. Lucky Duck.

THANK YOU!

Thank you for reading! If you enjoyed this book, please leave a review on Amazon, Goodreads, BookBub, The Story Graph, or anywhere else you like to track your recent reads. Alternatively, you could post online or tell a friend about it. This helps our authors more than you may know.

- The Team at Torchflame Books

ACKNOWLEDGMENTS

A true list of acknowledgments would feature a ridiculously long list of family, teachers, and coaches who have graced my life with their care and talents. More specifically, for this book, I do want to thank Clayton Short, a farmer from Assaria, Kansas, for help answering my agricultural questions, and Glen Williams, a high school friend who has spent a career in law enforcement, for his guidance about police protocols.

From the writing world, I thank Harlan Coben for his class that inspired me to finish this work and, most of all, my editor, the brilliant Chelsea Robinson, whose acumen has been needed and appreciated.

ABOUT THE AUTHOR

Mike Garretson's first experiences as a writer occurred when he was covering high school sports for local newspapers. After a career full of joy as a public school teacher, Mike has entered the arena of fiction writing. In *Lucky Duck*, Mike's debut novel, his love of sports and the 80s lifestyle comes through like frenzied crowds on a Black Friday before online shopping.

Mike will follow up this, not quite dark, "but a little gray" comedic adult fiction with two Middle Grade novels, *Stand-still* and *Eric the Great*.

Mike has always been a part of a big family. Trips to beaches and ballparks are his favorite activities when he ventures away from the small-town Kansas living he loves so much. You might find him working on the high school baseball field getting his teams ready to play or being involved in various community events. Mike encourages everyone to support their local and school libraries in any way they can along with local booksellers. You can connect with Mike on social media @MikeGwriting.